Sola Fidei
Bill Burgett
2009

THE CRUISE

by

Bill Burgett

McKenna Publishing Group
Indian Wells, California

The Cruise

ISBN: 1-932172-19-x
LCCN: 2004106987

First Edition
10 9 8 7 6 5 4 3 2 1
Printed in the United States of America

Visit us on the Web at: www.mckennapubgrp.com

Many thanks to Judy, my bride of forty-four years, Debbie Justis, my daughter and oldest child, and Carol Troestler, my rediscovered high school classmate and author, all of whom graciously read the rough draft of this book and provided valuable insights and welcome encouragement.

1

Frozen feelings. That was why Mark didn't laugh at jokes when everyone else was laughing or cry at funerals when everyone else was crying. It explained so much. Mark thought that he was different, maybe a little crazy, but the counselor helped him understand that he had been conditioned to suppress his feelings. It wasn't unusual for someone who had grown up in a troubled family, especially as an only child.

Now there was hope. He was experiencing a meltdown with Judy. He was feeling something. Was it love? He couldn't wait to be with her, to look at her, to touch her, to smell her. At the same time, he was afraid to yield to the new feelings. What if she didn't feel the same way? What if something happened to her?

Sergeant Mark Garrison met Judy Archer when he was investigating her husband's death. He was assigned the unwanted task of telling Judy that her husband's body had been found in the Des Plaines River. The coroner determined that Bob Archer, a well-known geneticist, had committed suicide. Throughout the investigation Judy found strength in Mark, and he became close to her. Respecting Judy's need to grieve, Mark kept his feelings in check. Now, a year later, Mark and Judy were in love and were planning to be married.

After high school Mark had entered the Army to become a military policeman. When his term of active duty was finished, he returned to Riverside, Illinois, and joined the Riverside Police Department. They paid for his academy training, but Mark wanted more. For the next four years he attended Riverside Community College on his own time and earned an Associate in Science degree in Law Enforcement. During his twelve years with the RPD he was promoted through the ranks to sergeant. Now he had his eyes on Lieutenant Corcoran's position, even though "Corky" was only slightly older than Mark. He was content to wait.

At thirty-six, Mark felt that he had made a breakthrough in his personal recovery, but now he was overwhelmed with new feelings and needed help. He knocked at the door of Jeff Myers, captain of the Riverside Police Department. Jeff invited Mark in with a wave of his hand.

"What's up, Mark?" Jeff asked.

"Jeff, do you remember a few years back when our medical insurance provided free personal counseling?"

"Sure, why?"

"Is that benefit still available?"

"As far as I know," Jeff answered. "Is the job getting to you, Mark? Sorry, I shouldn't have asked that."

"No," Mark answered. "Who could confirm that for me?"

"Ask Sue to call the insurance company."

Mark left Jeff's office without further discussion and walked to Sue's desk. Sue was the department clerk. "Sue, I need to know whether our medical insurance still covers the cost of personal counseling. Will you check that out and let me know?" Sue nodded without response, wondering but not asking.

After a few minutes Sue caught up with Mark who was sitting alone in the coffee room. "Five sessions is the limit, Mark. And you must use a counselor that accepts our insurance."

"Thanks, Sue." Mark knew who he would call—Doctor Gordon Lum. When the benefit was first announced, it was Dr. Lum who, in only five meetings, changed Mark's life. Now his life had taken a new turn. Now there was Judy and with her a whole new set of feelings. He needed help in sorting them out.

Dr. Lum specialized in addiction counseling. Thirty-something, slight in build and casually dressed, he greeted Mark at the side entrance of his house where he maintained his office. Softly lit by table lamps and smelling of coffee, the office was inviting. Lum motioned Mark to a cushioned chair and offered a drink. While the doctor poured coffee, Mark wondered how many tears had been shed on those chairs.

Mark felt good being in Dr. Lum's office again. It was here that he had received new life. When the Riverside Police Department first announced a counseling benefit it was understood that what was said would remain confidential and would not become part of the employee's record. Mark appreciated the benefit and the protection. He had always known that there was something missing in his life, but he had never been able to put a finger on it.

In his earlier meetings with Dr. Lum the counselor had seen through Mark's "presenting problem." Mark displayed all of the symptoms of a man suffering depression—joyless, unmotivated, feeling unappreciated—but Dr. Lum suspected something deeper. After Mark described his early life it didn't take long for the counselor to make a diagnosis. Mark was the typical product of troubled parents. Until he was eighteen and old enough to "escape" to the military, he had grown up as the only child of a workaholic father and an alcoholic mother. His father, a factory foreman, worked long hours and from a confused sense of self-pride refused to let his wife work outside the home. His mother, an accomplished writer, was abandoned in the suburbs without a car. His father expected her to be satisfied with household chores and single parenting, but it didn't work. Sheer boredom drove her to drink and then to seek companionship with other men. Neither parent had time for Mark. Both loved him in their own way, but the parenting voids were too great for healthy emotional development. Mark learned to stop sharing his feelings for fear of being ignored and, eventually, the stuffed feelings resulted in no feelings. It never dawned on him that this wasn't normal until he met Dr. Lum.

After several meetings Dr. Lum had Mark on the road to recovery. Lum introduced Mark to self-parenting books and gave him a list of support groups for adult children of alcoholics. Mark immersed himself in the books and began attending meetings. His greatest regret in the process was that both his parents had died—his father as a result of a heart attack and his mother from cirrhosis. There was no way for him to share his new appreciation for their struggles and their efforts to bring him up. He wished he could undo some of the anger and confusion that had defined him in his teen years, but that was no longer possible.

Now in Dr. Lum's office once again, Mark had new feelings. Judy Archer had opened new doors for him. Lum had explained in earlier meetings that Mark may never have as broad a range of emotional experiences as people raised in more "normal" circumstances. His "frozen feelings" may thaw some with help, but he would have to accept the fact that he could not return to his mother's womb and restart the process of growing up emotionally. Mark could accept this. Just knowing why he didn't laugh or cry when others did was helpful. His meetings helped him learn that he was not alone in this. Others shared this emotional vacuum, and others had gotten better. He would, too.

Now Judy stirred new feelings in him. Perhaps Dr. Lum would have more answers. He didn't. Lum smiled at Mark. "You've come a long way, Mark. What you are experiencing with Judy is not a result of your history. It is the common lot of people who have fallen in love. You are a late bloomer, to be sure, because of your history, but I am proud of the work that you have done since our last meetings. Now you have some catching up to do, and if Judy is the right girl for you she will help you do it." Dr. Lum stood and Mark realized that the meeting was over. He would have to deal with his new feelings on his own. In a sense, he had graduated from the school of Dr. Lum. Mark understood that he was now in the same boat with others that had been overwhelmed by love.

After meeting with Dr. Lum, Mark headed home by way of Marge's Diner. He had never learned to cook and hated to eat alone. Marge's, Burger King, and Dunkin' Donuts were his haunts. He knew that his "fast food" life would come to a fast end with Judy, but these places provided more than food. He had surrogate family here, and Marge was the head of the family.

"Well, look who's here—the prodigal son! Where have you been, Mark?" Marge asked from behind the counter.

"Around," said Mark, as he slid into a vinyl-covered booth. Marge's was the place where locals gathered, especially over morning coffee. She had kept the Diner open after her husband died, but both she and the Diner were showing signs of wear. Mark knew the menu and the specials by heart and ordered his favorite—meat loaf and mashed potatoes. There were only two other customers in the Diner, so Marge slipped into the booth beside Mark.

"I've missed you, Mark," she said.

"I know, Marge. I've been seeing someone. She makes pretty good meatloaf."

"You know how to hurt a girl, Mark," Marge said with a hint of a smile.

"I'll tell you the truth, Marge, I'm pretty serious about her."

"Well, it's about time, Mark Garrison," Marge chided. "A handsome guy like yourself should have been married off a long time ago. How'd you meet this meatloaf fraud?"

"She's Judy Archer. It was her husband that was found in the River last year."

"You mean the scientist from the city?" Marge asked.

"That's the one."

"When will I get to meet her? You can't marry her until I approve, you know!"

"Soon, Marge." Mark put his left arm around Marge's shoulder and gave her a hug. He didn't want to think about leaving Marge and the Diner behind when he made a new life with Judy. Marge turned away from Mark and got up to leave, but not before Mark saw the misting around her eyes. After dinner he headed home.

Home for Mark was the second floor of the Tetlow house. Ever since Mark returned to Riverside he had lived at the Tetlow's. Located in a residential neighborhood where two-family dwellings weren't permitted by zoning ordinance, the Tetlow's had evaded the ordinance by using a rear stairway as the main entrance to Mark's apartment. The stairs went up to a covered porch and from there one entered the kitchen. Mark was not a neatnik, but he had adopted his grandmother's slogan, "There's a place for everything, and everything in its place." Anyway, life was easier when you knew where things were. Past the kitchen was a hallway with the bathroom on the right, the only bedroom on the left, and a living room at the end. Mark's furniture was functional, uncoordinated, and like new, except for the recliner which showed signs of wear.

Mark removed his tweed sport coat, unfastened his shoulder holster, then placed both on the back of a chair in the kitchen. His telephone was on the kitchen counter tethered to an answering machine to its right, which was calling attention to itself by flashing its red light. The number two appeared on the screen. Mark decided to make himself a glass of iced tea before listening to the messages. He poured filtered water into a glass with the tea, added a dash of lemon juice, sat at one of two chairs near a round table, moved a pad of paper and pencil within reach, and pushed the play button on his answering machine. On hearing Judy's voice, the weariness of the day's work melted away and his mind snapped to attention.

"Hi. It's me. I just got home from school, and I'm now in a hot bath talking to a machine. How unromantic! I don't know what time you'll hear this, but if it's before dinner, would you be willing to drive into the city? I can't wait until the weekend to get together. I'll fix a late dinner for us. Call me and say you will."

The second call was a hang-up. Mark dialed Judy's number, but got a busy signal. She was probably on the Internet. It was already Thursday night. Saturday would come soon. They would have to wait. He would call her later.

Although they had agreed to marry, Mark and Judy had deferred making definite plans. At thirty-six, Mark knew that the clock was running down if he and Judy were to have a family. He wanted a family. He wanted to experience what life might be like in a normal family. He wanted to coach his boy's teams and walk a daughter down the aisle. Whether he would enjoy grandchildren would depend on when he and Judy got started, but he hoped for that, too. He also knew that life would be different. Judy was used to marriage. She and Bob had been married for years. This was new for him. He was comfortable with his life. But now he couldn't imagine life without Judy. Dr. Lum's words were both encouraging and challenging. This was not a problem of frozen feelings. It was the common lot of lovers, but somehow that didn't ease the uncertainty of merging two lives.

Mark took his iced tea into the living room and collapsed in his recliner. He would like to have started a fire in the fireplace, but it was May and there was no fireplace on the second floor of the Tetlow house. One of the few good memories of his turbulent upbringing was of nights in front of the fireplace. He could shut out the drunken slurs of his mother or the blaring of the radio and lay in front of the fireplace watching the flames leaping up to the flue. Sometimes he felt like the logs; felt as though he, too, would disappear over time and become invisible in his own home. Hanging above the fireplace was an old seascape. Waves crashed against the rocks in the foreground while on the horizon a sailing ship sat in calm water. Even as a boy, Mark longed to get past the tumult of his life and find calmer waters. The ringing of the phone startled him. Forcing himself out of his recliner, he got to the kitchen just in time to beat the answering machine. "Hello."

"Hi. It's me," Judy said.

"I tried calling you back, but the line was busy," Mark said.

"I was talking to my mother. I needed to talk to someone tonight."

"How is she doing?" Mark asked.

"She's okay. We didn't talk long."

"After work I saw Dr. Lum, then had dinner at Marge's."

"Dr. Lum?" Judy was surprised that Mark hadn't spoken of seeing Dr. Lum sooner.

"It was a good meeting, Judy. I'll tell you more about it on Saturday."

"I know it's too late to get together tonight, but I don't know if I can wait until Saturday."

"I want to see you, too, but I have a full day tomorrow, and a session at the firing range tomorrow night. Want to go with me to the range?" Mark asked.

Judy hadn't been to a firing range since Bob had insisted that she learn how to use the pistol that he bought, ostensibly, for her protection—the same pistol with which he had taken his life. The thought of the firing range awakened memories that she did not want awakened. "I haven't been to a range since Bob taught me to fire his .22," she answered. "I'd rather not, if you don't mind."

"I'm sorry, Judy. It was thoughtless. Let's stick to our plans for Saturday, okay?"

"I hope you're ready for a very needy lady," Judy responded.

"I love you, Judy."

"You'd better."

Mark woke up in his recliner. He hated it when that happened. He was stiff and his clothes were wrinkled. Cleaned up and changed, he headed for the Y. Monday, Wednesday, and Friday were workout days at the Riverside Y. The Army had gotten Mark into the habit of regular physical training, but it was Captain Myers who kept the habit alive. He insisted that the Riverside police force stay in shape, and Mark understood that a cop out of condition was a cop in trouble. He had a routine beginning on the treadmill, then some isometrics on the pneumatic equipment, then a swim. On the way out of the Y he would stop at the health bar for a fruit drink, then head for Dunkin' Donuts to get a dozen assorted for the office.

"Hi, Sue," he said as he passed by the clerk's desk. Sue had been with the force longer than Mark. Because Mark didn't like to take notes or write reports, she transcribed his microcassette tapes. This was not in her job description, but she did it as a courtesy. As a result, she knew every detail of Mark's work. And Mark acknowledged her extra effort at birthdays and holidays. "Whose new Beemer is that in the parking lot?" Mark asked.

"Mine," Sue answered.

"Rich relative die?" Mark asked, knowing what Sue earned on the force.

"Not exactly," Sue answered without further comment. Mark didn't pursue the issue.

"Is Corky in?" Mark asked.

"Not yet."

Mark took the donuts to the coffee room, poured a cup, capped it and headed for the front door.

"Sign me out, Sue. I'm going to see if I can dig up Ed Braun."

Everyone in Riverside knew Ed Braun. Injured in a high school accident, he was partly disabled. To add to his SSI income he did part-time work at the train station. Mark liked Ed. He was a straight shooter who knew everything that was going on in town. When Dr. Bob Archer's body was found under a fishing pier in the Des Plaines River it was Ed Braun who knew the river and its currents and suggested to Mark that Archer had taken a dive or fallen off of the railroad bridge. That's where they found Archer's pistol.

Although Bob Archer's death was ruled a suicide, the circumstances leading up to it had colossal implications for his company, Bio-Gen, and for Judy Archer. Even though the Archer case was closed as a police matter, there was still the matter of missing evidence, stolen from the police department while in Mark's custody, a matter that Mark couldn't dismiss.

Archer was a renowned geneticist working on the Human Genome Project. In the course of his work he had discovered a gene defect common to every human sample of DNA that he tested. Archer knew that a common mutation is an anomaly. Without authorization he digressed from his assigned work and devoted his time and his company's time to develop a way to repair the defective gene. His remedy worked on two human subjects, but Archer couldn't advance the project because his experiments violated scientific and legal protocol. Nevertheless, he had made an amazing discovery.

The remedy developed by Archer improved the mental, physical, and spiritual conditions of his two human subjects, but when Archer took his life and the treatment was no longer available, both subjects reverted to their former conditions and died. The only existing records of Archer's work were on ZIP disks, but these disks had been stolen from the police department. Mark had placed them in the evidence lockup for safekeeping, but during a monthly inventory of the lockup Sue reported that she had moved the box containing the disks to Mark's office for better identification. The cleanup crew placed the box in a trash container behind the police station, but when questioned the crew that picked up the trash did not recall seeing the box. It was assumed that trash raiders had taken the box.

Mark and Judy were anxious about the whereabouts of Archer's evidence because his covert work had resulted in his suicide, the murder of his assistant, and the arrest and conviction of the killers. Because the disks had been in his custody, Mark felt responsible for finding them and bringing closure to the Archer affair. He was "off the clock" according to Captain Myers since the Archer case was officially closed, but Mark would not quit until the disks were located. Perhaps Ed Braun could help.

As arranged, Ed was at Marge's Diner eating a late breakfast when

Mark joined him at the counter. "Breakfast, Mark?" Marge asked as she poured coffee into his cup.

"Fruit drink at the Y, Marge," Mark answered. "Coffee will do for now."

Ed acknowledged Mark with a wave of his fork. "What's up, Mark?" he asked.

"Any luck on the disks, Ed?" Mark asked, certain that Ed would have called if he had discovered anything. Only a few people knew the contents of the disks, and Ed Braun wasn't one of them. All he had been told was that disks related to the case had been stolen from the trash behind the police department.

Ed shook his head while negotiating a bite of his pancakes. "Nope," he mumbled.

"Have you got any ideas as to who might have taken them, Ed?" Mark asked.

"Yep, but the guy I would have suspected was in your drunk cell on the night they were taken," Ed replied. "I don't have anyone else in mind."

"How about the clean-up crew at the station?" Mark asked. "Could it be one of their people?"

"I'll check around, but I doubt it," Ed answered. "They are good folks who have too much to lose, especially by taking something from the police station, but I'll check around some more. Why are you so interested in these disks?"

"Want to close the case," is all that Mark would offer.

"How's Ed?" Sue asked as Mark returned to the office.

"Same as always," Mark answered.

"Are you still chasing the disks?" Sue asked.

"Yep. Not going to stop till I find them," Mark said.

"Lost cause," said Sue. "You have better things to do. They're long gone."

"What do you mean, Sue?" Mark asked.

"I mean whoever has them has no idea what's on them and probably wouldn't know what to do with them anyway." Sue knew what the disks contained since she had transcribed all of Mark's notes regarding the Archer case. She knew the importance of the disks. Perhaps she was right. Maybe they were tossed into a ditch somewhere and would never be found, but he was not going to assume anything.

"Perhaps you're right, Sue," Mark responded, "but you know what's on them and how important they are to a lot of people. I'm sure you can understand why I'm interested."

Sue didn't respond, but turned to her keyboard and resumed her work.

That evening Mark met his monthly obligation at the firing range, but his heart wasn't in it. Judy was on his mind. In a real life situation he would have missed his target altogether and would be lying dead on the street. He cleaned his pistol and left the range. Tomorrow he and Judy would shop for rings.

Thrifty by nature, Mark had saved a lot of money. The cost wasn't as important to Mark as the symbolic meaning of the rings. This was real commitment. Tomorrow he would be making a decision that would change everything. Marrying Judy was a given. He loved her with his whole being and wanted nothing more than to spend the rest of his life with her, but Mark had worked hard to make the life that he had. Dr. Lum was right when he said Mark had come a long way, but there was much about him that Judy didn't know and there was much about Judy that he didn't know. Would they ever truly know each other? Wasn't there something to be said for the adventure of discovery? Did he need to know more or tell more in order to love Judy more? Did Judy need more time to deal with Bob's death and the whole mess that followed? Would the missing disks stand between them? Would she hold him accountable for their loss? Was he searching for reasons to avoid a commitment? Perhaps every man went through this kind of questioning before tying the knot.

By the time Mark arrived home from the firing range it was too late to call Judy. She would be in bed and Mark's mind was swimming from his work, the uncertainty about the disks, and what Dr. Lum called "living inside his head." He twisted the top off of a Sam Adams and settled into his recliner to watch the late news. Determined not to fall asleep in the recliner again, he forced himself to sit upright. After the news he went to bed, but sleep was intermittent.

• • •

The skim milk in Mark's refrigerator was past the expired date and tasted sour. He dumped it into the sink and settled for a cup of coffee. At 8:00 A.M. he called Judy. She had been working out on her NordicRider. "Ready to go shopping for rings?" he asked.

"I've been ready for a long time," she quipped. "When are you coming to get me?"

"I'm out of breakfast food. I'd like to stop by Denny's and eat. Have you had breakfast?"

"A bagel and fruit juice, but I would rather watch you eat than sit at home," she said.

"I'll pick you up in about an hour," Mark said. Judy lived a half-hour away from Riverside in the townhouse that she had shared with Bob. Together they had restored the townhouse, but as nice as it was Mark hoped that Judy would be willing to move after they were married. He didn't believe in ghosts, but he also didn't think that anyone could forget the memories that a house contained. Bob and Judy had gone over every inch of the townhouse—stripping, staining, papering, tiling, and so on—side by side. There was no place that Judy could go that she wouldn't hear Bob's voice or share his joy as the house was transformed from neglected old age to elegant youth. And, as functional as the Tetlow's second floor had been for Mark, it was no place to start a family. In contrast to Judy's tasteful furnishings Mark's place was stark. The décor was early bachelor. The subject of where to live hadn't come up and Mark didn't think that he was ready to raise it.

Mark shaved, showered, and dressed for the day. He was always well groomed and practically dressed. Fashions didn't interest him, but his military and police background had instilled in him a respect for neatness and a clean-shaven appearance. His closets were not crowded, but the clothes that he had were clean, tailored, and appropriate for his age. With his athletic build, six foot, one inch height, and 190 pound frame, he could wear clothes right off of the rack. Mark's hair was cut short, but laid flat with a left-side part. There was a hint of gray around the edges. He had a square-jawed face and his smile had the hint of mischief.

As Mark drove to Judy's, he pictured his family-to-be going on an outing in the unmarked police car. He could imagine his children playing with the emergency switches and fingering the loaded shotgun. It was clear that they would need a new car. Judy's old Escort wouldn't be big enough and she had sold Bob's Taurus after his death. Another decision, but one that would have to wait.

Kelly, Judy's Welsh Corgi, recognized Mark's car at once and rose to his feet as Mark pulled into the parking place in front of Judy's townhouse. Judy got up from the front steps and met Mark with a hug and a lingering kiss. Kelly, too old to jump up on his short legs, dribbled in excitement and wagged his tail. "Let me take the dog inside and get my purse, and I'll be right back," she said. Mark waited by the car.

"How was the firing range last night?" Judy asked as she climbed into the passenger's seat.

"Couldn't hit the side of a barn," Mark replied.

"Something on your mind?" she asked.

"Someone," he answered.

"Anyone I know?" she said with a smile.

The jewelry stores didn't open until ten, so Mark had a leisurely breakfast at Denny's. "You know what I'd like to do after we're done shopping?" Judy asked, not needing an answer. "I'd like to go back to my place, put on a Johnny Mathis CD, and dance."

"Who could argue with a plan like that?" Mark said with a smile.

"Remember what happened the last time we did that?" she asked.

"It seems to me that you proposed," he said.

"I just anticipated the question. If you're feeling trapped, I suppose you'll just have to take me back to my place so that I can start looking for another victim."

"I don't mind being trapped," Mark said.

"What's next?" Mark asked after they had finished shopping for rings. He had not been through the marriage drill before, and needed a plan of action for the event.

"Next we go to my townhouse," Judy answered.

"I mean what's the next step in our marriage plans," Mark clarified.

"Next, we have to sit down with a wedding planner and put together a schedule of things to be done," Judy said, "but first let's go back to my place and relax."

"You do realize that I don't have much experience at this sort of thing," Mark said.

"I know that, Mark," Judy said, "and because I do this will not be the blowout it was when I married Bob. Not because it was Bob, but because it was my first marriage. Our wedding will be more modest. Do you agree with that?" He nodded. It was exactly what Mark had been wanting, but he was glad that Judy had said it. "There's time for us to do the wedding planning," Judy said. "We've done all that we need to do for today." When they arrived at the townhouse, Judy went upstairs to change.

Wineglasses were on the kitchen counter and a Johnny Mathis CD was on a table next to the entertainment center in the living room. Mark put the CD in the player and sat down in a cushioned chair as the words of *Warm* began to warm the house. He didn't hear Judy come down but felt her hands sliding over his shoulders as she stood behind him. She laid her head on his shoulder and they remained silent while Johnny Mathis transported them to another world. They danced their way through the CD with few words shared. Judy's feet barely touched the ground. She had never dreamed that she would feel this way again. It had been years since the romance had gone out of her marriage with Bob. When the CD ended, they ate a light dinner in the kitchen.

"You make my life complete, Judy," Mark said, not knowing where the words came from. He was indulging himself in a flood of new feelings. "You're the best thing that's happened to me."

Judy knew that Mark had never been married, but she never asked whether he had been in love. "Have you ever been in love, Mark?"

"Yes, once," he said, "to a girl in junior high school, but her father moved her family across the country to California. I thought my life had ended."

"Puppy love," Judy said.

"Didn't seem like it at the time," Mark responded. "My heart was broken."

"Anyone since then?" she asked.

"Nothing serious," he answered. "Why the third degree?"

"I suddenly realized that I don't know much about you," she said.

"I don't know much about you, either," Mark said.

Judy got up from the table without a word and began to gather the dishes. "It's late, Mark, and you should probably go. Besides, I want to attend early church tomorrow."

Surprised that the evening had ended so abruptly, Mark got up from the table, gave Judy a hug, then left. He didn't understand what had happened. In one minute their blissful evening had ended and he had been sent home. Although making progress with his feelings, Judy's dismissal hit a nerve. His fear of rejection was always just under the surface and this had seemed like rejection. Before Dr. Lum he would have crawled into a hole, but now he wanted to understand what had happened. As soon as he got to his apartment he called Judy. The minute he said hello she apologized.

"Mark, I am terribly sorry about ending our evening the way I did. There is no way that you can understand what happened. I'm not ready for show-and-tell. There are things about me that you don't know and I'm afraid to tell you for fear of losing you."

"Judy, in a few days you are going to wear an engagement ring. That means that soon you will be my wife. That's not because you've passed some kind of qualifying exam. We're going to be married, raise beautiful children, and grow old together. All I want is to spend the rest of my life with you."

Judy couldn't speak through her tears. She gently placed the phone in the cradle. Normally Kelly wasn't allowed on the furniture, but after Mark's call Judy lifted the old dog into her bed, and with Kelly lying quietly at her side she let the tears flow.

She knew it would happen and she had only herself to blame. She had opened the conversation with her stupid question about Mark's love life. Delving into the past was too risky at this stage of their relationship. He would find out soon enough. He would have to find out. He wanted children and that wasn't going to happen. He looked forward to a long, happy life. She hoped that she could give him that. God knows she loved him more than she had ever loved any man. It had been different with Bob. Bob knew. She married Bob because he was safe. He understood.

Judy first learned about Bob Archer in an article in a science magazine. He was a renowned geneticist working part-time with a team of scientists trying to locate the genetic source of Huntington's Disease. It was known that Huntington's was passed from one generation to another. Judy's biological father, Richard Hammond, had died of Huntington's when Judy was eleven, and she had lived through the worst of his suffering. She knew that she had a fifty-percent chance of having the same genetic defect. Since the symptoms usually show up in midlife there was only one way of knowing whether she had the disease—to be tested, but knowing wasn't all that it was cracked up to be.

Judy remembered the day she first met Bob. He was lecturing in the city just an hour from the apartment that she shared with another high school teacher. She attended Bob's lecture and was excited to learn that the research team was getting close to locating the genetic source and, consequently, a diagnostic test for identifying the disease. There were very few people in the audience so it wasn't difficult for Judy to meet Dr. Archer. Since Huntington's is a relatively rare disease he was pleased to meet a member of a Huntington's family. Judy became a subject of his research study. They met several times in his office where Judy underwent neurological tests to establish a base line history for herself, but Dr. Archer was mainly interested in her family history. His associate led Judy through a genealogical history tracing her roots as far back as she could remember.

After their final meeting, Dr. Archer asked Judy to have dinner with him. He was young, bright, and handsome. She accepted and one thing led to another. Marrying Bob Archer was safe. He had no illusions about children. There would be none. She might have Huntington's Disease which would mean that her children would have a fifty-percent chance of having it, too. She would not expose anyone to what her father had suffered. The images of his final years were still vivid in her mind.

When the defective gene that causes Huntington's was discovered and the diagnostic test was established, Bob Archer was recruited by Bio-Gen, a laboratory contracted by the NIH to do research on the Human Genome Project.

2

The morning May sun was shining brightly through the French doors of Judy's bedroom. She awoke to Kelly's whines. The dog was too old and her legs were too short to jump to the floor, so he whined in short, high-pitched bursts, growing progressively louder. Judy rolled over and put her arm around the old dog. She lay there for awhile planning how she would make things up to Mark for cutting off their evening and their phone conversation. She didn't have long to plan.

True to his breed, Kelly had remarkable hearing. He heard Mark's car pull up to the townhouse and started barking in the ear-splitting bark of a Welsh Corgi. Judy lifted him off of the bed, slipped into a robe and slippers, and went to the front door. Without a word, she thrust her hand through the partially opened front door and handed Kelly's leash to Mark. Kelly slipped through the door to do his business.

Mark had never seen Judy at wakeup time. She had run her hands through her hair but had not had time to put on her makeup. She was a natural beauty. With or without makeup she did not look thirty-four years old. Working out regularly on her NordicRider, walking or jogging when she could, and getting enough rest to stay alert and productive helped her guard her looks and her health. She had never smoked or used drugs but occasionally had a glass of white Port, usually after a hectic day of teaching. Clothes were not an obsession for her, but like Mark she was well groomed and modestly fashionable. When doing her housework she often shed her clothes completely, enjoying the freedom of her body. Bob Archer had been attracted to blondes with long hair, so Judy was accustomed to having her hair cut to shoulder length. At 126 pounds and five-feet, seven inches tall, she could pass for a woman ten years younger.

Judy bent to unfasten Kelly's leash and her robe fell partly open at the top. Reluctantly, Mark averted his gaze. He wanted nothing more than to take her in his arms and make love to her, but that would wait until the wedding night. Judy held marriage sacred, and Mark did not wish to offend her principles. After releasing the dog, Judy stepped closer to Mark and, putting her hands on his shoulders, drew him into her. Their kiss said everything that needed to be said. No further mention was made of the events of the previous night.

Mark was in Levi's and a cotton, long-sleeved shirt suitable for the chill of the May morning. It was too late for Judy to make early church, so they had bagels and coffee in her kitchen, then she prepared for late church. "Why don't you come with me?" she asked.

"I'm hardly dressed for church," Mark noted, although his clothes were clean and neat.

"We're not that formal at church. Some men wear suits, others are more casual," she said. "Pastor Dressler's sermons are a little dry, but his message is clear. You might like it." Mark agreed to go.

In his capacity as a policeman, Mark had become acquainted with Scott Dressler. Bob Archer's work at Bio-Gen had implications for the church at large, and Scott Dressler, after a confidential conversation with Judy Archer following Bob's suicide, had violated her confidence by discussing Archer's work with a colleague. His disclosure had serious results. Dressler had begged Judy's forgiveness for his indiscretion and received it. Judy continued to worship at Dressler's church because of his Bible classes. He was very bright, did good research, and was an excellent teacher.

The Reverend Scott Dressler's sermon on the post-resurrection appearances of Jesus impressed Mark who didn't go in for showy preaching. Dressler's sermon was well organized, well presented, and it was clear by his manner that he believed what he preached. During his years in the military Mark had attended a Protestant chapel several times but had come away with more questions than answers. On the other hand, Judy was a committed Christian. Her mother had seen to it that Judy was baptized and attended Sunday school. She began confirmation studies in the year that her mother married Donald Douglas and was confirmed on Palm Sunday in the eighth grade. After the death of her father and the remarriage of her mother, more attention was focused on Judy and she was happier than she had ever been. Donald Douglas was a widower when he met Judy's mother and had no children by his first wife. He was good to her mother and loved Judy as his own. Judy loved him and loved life. As a confirmation gift, her mother and Donald took her out to dinner where Donald announced that he would like to adopt Judy. She agreed, and by her freshman year in high school Judy Hammond became Judy Douglas, and Donald became Dad.

While active in youth group activities, Judy made her decision to become a high school teacher. After graduating from college magna cum laude, she received her state certification and was hired to teach English to high school seniors. She had respect for her students, especially those who shared her love for the language.

Reverend Dressler asked Judy more than once to teach an adult Bible class, but she declined, not because she didn't love the subject, but because she needed a break from the lectern. "When are we going to get you into the classroom, Judy?" he asked again as she and Mark were exiting the sanctuary.

"Perhaps in time, Pastor, but I have another agenda just now. Mark and I are going to be married."

"I hope you are planning to be married here, Judy," he said, remembering how he had let her down in the Archer affair.

"Of course, Pastor Dressler," she said with friendly enthusiasm.

"When is the wedding planned?" Dressler asked.

"We're working on that, and you'll be the first to know," she said with a smile as she and Mark moved past the minister.

Reluctantly, Judy told Mark that she would have to go home from the church to grade papers. As they drove Mark began to ask questions about her faith. "I've never been much of a churchgoer as you know, Judy," he said, "and I'm not sure how to catch up on what I've missed. You know so much about your faith and I know so little."

"It's not too late to start learning, Mark," she said trying to find a level of encouragement that would not push him too hard. Inside she was aglow with hope.

"As far as I know I haven't been baptized," he said.

"It might be best for you to join Pastor Dressler's instruction class," she suggested.

"Is it for adults?" he asked.

"Yes, it's for adults." Smiling, she reached across the radio equipment and touched his hand.

"Would you attend the class with me?" he appealed.

"I'd like nothing better," she assured.

"I'll do it," he said. Judy was beside herself.

She said goodbye to Mark at the curbside, and they agreed to begin doing wedding planning on the following Friday evening. After taking Kelly out to do his business, Judy undressed and slipped into a tee shirt and shorts. She put some classical CD's on the turntable, turned the volume low, and climbed barefoot into the love seat in her living room. Sitting yoga style, she tried to empty her mind to begin reading her students' papers. Memories of the weekend would not go away. She knew that Mark's expectations of their marriage and what she could deliver were on a collision course. Perhaps their faith could get them through what lay ahead. Kelly curled up at the foot of the love seat and Judy reached for the first paper.

Judy should have been reading more final papers, but she couldn't. The thought of her mother and her biological father, Richard Hammond, kept coming to mind. She had never known him when he wasn't sick. From the time that she could remember, he had been different with his shaking and depression. He always seemed to know what was going on, but he was forgetful, and awkward. Judy was afraid of him, although he told her often how much he loved her and wished he could do things with her. Judy wasn't allowed to discuss her father outside of the house, and his disease was never mentioned within the family. It wasn't until after he died when Judy was eleven that her mother explained about Huntington's Disease, including that Judy herself might have the disease. She decided to call her mother.

"Hello," Lois answered in a tired voice.

"Hi, Mom," Judy said.

"It's been a long time since you've called, Judy," her mother said with a slight tone of reproof.

"I'm sorry, Mom. I have no excuse, I know, but I've been spending all of my spare time with Mark."

"Are you going to marry Mark?" her mother asked.

"That's one of the reasons I'm calling. We've ordered the rings and talked to the Pastor."

"Have you been tested, Judy?"

It saddened Judy that this had to be her mother's first question. In most families a question about whether she loved Mark or when the marriage was planned would be first. It was a reminder of the black cloud that would never go away. "No," she answered, expecting advice.

"Mark isn't Bob, Judy," her mother said. "Mark needs to know. You are at the age when Huntington shows up. In fact, you're older than some. What will happen if you don't tell him and the symptoms start? Won't he feel deceived?"

"I love him, Mom, just like you must have loved Dad. Did you know that he had Huntington's?"

"I only knew that his father had died, and that one of his father's brothers had died before I met Richard. There was no mention of Huntington's Disease. No one told me that the disease was hereditary. I'm not even sure that they knew. It was called Huntington's Chorea at that time, and it was relatively unstudied. Now they know how to test for it. Yes, I loved Richard, but we weren't married long before his symptoms began, right about the time that I got pregnant with you. Life after that was a nightmare. You must get tested, Judy."

"I can't bear the thought of losing Mark, Mom."

"Your marriage will be built on a lie, Judy."

"Not if I don't have the disease. One of every two children escape it."

"You could know for certain."

"And what if I test positive?"

"Then you will have to leave it up to Mark whether you get married."

"I don't want to live in terror, paranoid every time I stumble or forget something, thinking that this is it."

"Then don't. Live one day at a time. Make the most of each day with Mark, if he's willing to marry."

"He wants children," Judy said.

"Of course he does," her mother replied. "He loves you and wants to have a normal, happy family. That may be possible for you, Judy, if you do not have the disease, but only testing will tell. If you are free of the disease, you can have children without any fear. Huntington's does not skip generations."

"Mom, I'd like to bring Mark up for a visit."

"We'd love to have you. Donald and I will not discuss Huntington's unless you bring it up. You have my promise. Let us know when you're coming. I love you, Judy."

"I love you, too, Mom."

Judy got into her Escort and drove to Mark's apartment. She had only been there once before, and she had waited in Mark's car while he went inside. This time she took the chance that he'd be home and went unannounced. The weeknight visit surprised Mark, but he was delighted and greeted her with a hug. "Wow," he said, "this is a first."

"I couldn't stay focused on my work," she said. "Besides, there is something we need to discuss."

"I have something to tell you, too, Judy." She was glad for the distraction.

"You go first," she said.

"I met with Pastor Dressler today," Mark said. "We decided that I should begin attending church and getting to know the people there. Then, if I wish, he will get me enrolled in a course of instruction. He suggested that you could be my mentor. Would you? It would mean much more to me if we could do this thing together."

Judy didn't know what to say. She just stared at Mark. Then the tears began to flow. She sat down at the kitchen table, her head in her hands, and sobbed. Mark was surprised at her reaction to his news and sat beside her not knowing what to do. He put his hand on her head, and sat quietly until she regained her composure. Strength flowed from his hand to her heart. She could recall the first time she met Mark. He had come to her townhouse to tell her that Bob's body had been found in the River. She was overcome and needed support. Mark had held her then and she had felt his strength. Now, ready to tell Mark about her family history, she needed his strength again, but Mark had derailed her. He was so excited about exploring his faith and partnering with her in the process, that she could not bring herself to talk about Huntington's. "Of course, I'll go through the instruction with you," she said, turning misty eyes toward Mark.

"I want us to set the right example for our children," Mark said, "and who knows? It might fill a void in my life."

"That's a given," said Judy, "but you'll have to discover that as you grow. Faith is a very personal thing. I'll mentor your studies, but you'll develop your own relationship with God."

"Why did you come tonight, Judy?" Mark asked, aware that he had dominated the conversation.

Judy said, "I talked to my mother this evening. She and Dad want to meet you. I thought that we should plan a trip to see them. You will love them, and they will love you. Are you willing?"

"Of course. Is this the part where I get the once-over?" he quipped.

"Yes. And Dad is very protective. You might want to bring your gun," she said.

"I suppose I'll have to ask for your hand," Mark said, half seriously.

"I told Mom that you probably would," said Judy.

"When do we go?" Mark asked.

"ASAP," Judy replied.

"Drive or fly?" Mark asked.

"Let's fly up as soon as school is out," Judy said.

"Done deal," Mark answered. "Will you make the arrangements?" Judy agreed.

"It's late, Mark. I've got to go home."

Mark walked her to her car, kissed her before opening her car door, and waited at the curb until she pulled away.

As she drove home, Judy's thoughts were conflicted. On the one hand, she should have been encouraged by Mark's decision to explore his faith and his desire to establish a church-going family. On the other hand, she had not told him that she might have a disease that would preclude children and end in her premature death. She would follow her mother's advice and take one day at a time.

3

An early riser, George Palmer, supervisor of product research at Bio-Gen Laboratories, was at the lab by 6:00 A.M. As he approached his office he heard his phone ringing. It could only be an emergency call. Bio-Gen didn't open officially until 8:30 A.M. He fumbled for his keys and opened his office door just as the phone rang a second time. Grabbing for the handset before the answering machine could kick in, George said a breathless, "Hello."

"Good morning, George," the voice on the other end replied. "Are you ready for some good news?"

"If it's going to cost me as much as the last time, I'm not sure," George answered.

"The last time you heard from *me*. Are you ready to hear from Dr. Archer?" the caller asked.

"You can raise the dead?" George asked.

"Second best, George. I have the disks. Interested?"

George sat down. "Those disks were stolen and never recovered. They were located in Bloomington, Illinois, and were reformatted in a pawn-shop and sold. What are you trying to pull? Archer's assistant never made the backups I requested before they were stolen, and now you tell me that you have them? What kind of scam are you trying to pull?"

"Easy, George. I've already told you about Gene 15105 and Dr. Archer's moonlighting. You must have believed what I told you. Your payment was very generous. Now, it's time to do some more business."

The caller had been paid $50,000 for information about Dr. Archer's clandestine work. George had learned that Dr. Archer had discovered a universal defect in Gene 15105 and a remedy for the defect. He knew about the human trials on a death row prisoner named Harley and a drug addict named Barbara Arnold, both now dead. He also had been told that the ZIP disks on which this work was recorded had been destroyed, thus ending any risk to Bio-Gen. Had Dr. Archer's work become public knowledge, Bio-Gen's multi-million dollar contract as a partner lab in the Human Genome Project would have been in jeopardy. NIH would have dropped them like a hot potato. George had begun to put the Archer nightmare out of his mind. "What exactly do you have, and where did you get it?" George asked.

"I have twenty-two ZIP disks. Eighteen contain data. Four contain text. Trust me, George, the text disks are very interesting." The caller emphasized "very." "If you want them, you'll have to pay another installment."

"What do you mean installment?" George asked.

"First, let's talk about the text disks," the caller said. "If you find them interesting, as I have, you may want to do more shopping. Understand?"

"What is your price?" George asked.

"$25,000 for each of the four text disks, then we'll discuss the others."

"I'll have to get back to you," George replied.

"Nice try, George. I'll get back to you tomorrow, but not at this number." The phone went dead.

Mark stopped by Marge's Diner on the way to the station. He was looking for Ed Braun. "Hi, Mark," Marge called across the counter. "Regular?" she asked.

"Already ate at home, Marge. I'm looking for Ed. Has he been in yet this morning?"

"Nope. Try the station," Marge answered.

"Later," Mark called as he left the diner. He drove to the train station. The station was like many built on the long line of tracks that connected the city with the northwestern suburbs, but most of them had been replaced with rain shelters. The station in Riverside, however, had been left standing. Ed Braun was the reason. He kept the old building in repair. Mark called his name as he approached from behind. "Hey, Ed."

"Hi, Mark," Ed replied. "Going to the city?"

"Not here for the train, Ed. Can we go inside and talk?" Ed stood on the platform until the train pulled away, then followed Mark into what had been the cab dispatcher's office."What's up, Mark?" Ed asked.

"I'm following up on the Archer disks, Ed. Have you come up with anything?"

"Sorry, Mark, but none of the 'regulars' claim to know anything about the disks." The regulars were the transients who hung around Riverside. During the warm weather most lived in out-of-sight shacks or makeshift tents in the woods along the Des Plaines River. Ed had put the word out about the missing disks, but no one claimed to know about them.

"Would they tell you if they did?" Mark asked.

"Probably. Trash raiding is not a crime. Most of the transients are decent people, just down on their luck, as they say."

Mark thought that he would want Ed as a friend if he were ever down on his luck. "Ed, one more thing. Would you follow up with the crew that cleans up at the police station? Just in case they might have forgotten something. Sue can give you the names of the crew that was on duty the night they were taken."

"Sure thing, Mark."

Mark wouldn't think of insulting Ed with a gift of money. "By the way, Ed, I left a package in your pickup," Mark shouted over his shoulder as he got into his police vehicle.

Curious, Ed walked to his old F-150 and pulled a long package wrapped in brown paper out of the body. It was an ultra-light fishing rod with a Garcia spinning reel. Mark was long gone, but Ed waved his hand in the direction Mark had taken.

Judy was eager to see her parents and to introduce them to Mark. Judy knew that he had picked up the rings. She had tried hers on and they fit perfectly. Mark was going to do things the traditional way, so he put the rings in his pocket. As anxious as Judy was to wear the engagement ring, she was also flattered by his romantic approach. She would follow his lead. In truth, Mark hadn't formally proposed.

The flight took only ninety minutes. It seemed as though they had barely reached cruising altitude when they began their descent. Judy's parents were standing in the main terminal when Mark and Judy approached. Mark wondered how they would accept him. His concerns were quickly forgotten as Judy's parents stretched out their arms and embraced them both.

"Don Douglas, and my wife, Lois," Judy's father said as he reached for Mark's shoulders and pulled Mark's large body down in a hug. Mark was not a hugger, but he placed his arms around Don's shoulders and tried not to hurt the older man. Lois Douglas did one better. She gave Mark a hug, then kissed him on his cheek. Judy stepped back so that Mark wouldn't see her laugh.

After the luggage was deposited in Judy's old bedroom, Mark kicked off his shoes, laid down on top of the quilt, then fell asleep. Judy quietly slipped out of the bedroom and went to the kitchen where her mother was preparing lunch. "Have you talked to Dad about Richard?" she asked.

"What about Richard?" her mother asked.

"Mom, it is important to me that Mark not know about Richard now," Judy answered.

"I'm sorry, Judy. I forgot. Yes, of course, we'll do as you ask. But you know that you can't keep it from him forever. To answer your question, no, I haven't discussed this with Donald."

"Will you do it now before Mark wakes up?" Judy pleaded.

"If you'll finish preparing lunch." Lois left the kitchen in search of Donald, while Judy stirred the soup. She was back in less than five minutes.

"Donald agrees to let you be the one to tell Mark about your family," Lois reported, "but, he also agrees with me that you should be honest with Mark. You don't want a marriage built on a lie, Judy."

"I don't know what I want, Mom," Judy confessed.

Lois took Judy in her arms and held her. They were still holding one another quietly when Mark entered the kitchen. "Am I interrupting?" he asked.

"No, come in, Mark," Judy said.

"I apologize for conking out," he said. "Can I help with anything?"

"No, we're okay. Why don't you keep Dad company," Judy answered. Judy's father was in the den, reclining in front of the TV. The History

Channel was showing a Civil War segment on the Battle of the Wilderness. "May I join you?" Mark asked. Don motioned to a matching recliner and Mark sat down. "I'd like to speak to you privately, sir, if we can set some time aside," Mark said.

"How about now?" Don said, anticipating what Mark was going to ask. He reached for the remote control and shut off the TV.

"Fine. I know that we don't know each other very well, and I would like to be able to spend more time with you, but considering the distance between us, I..."

Don interrupted in the middle of Mark's sentence. "You may have my daughter's hand in marriage, Mark," he said. "Judy has told us all we need to know about you. You have made her very happy. We trust her judgment, and her happiness is all we seek for her. You have our blessing."

"I had my speech all prepared," Mark said with a broad smile. "You've made it easy for me. Be sure, I will love her and care for her."

"Marriage has its challenges, Mark. It is for better and for worse, but I think that you're right for her. When do you plan to pop the question?" Donald asked.

"We've already discussed marriage. I have the rings with me now, and I may ask her tonight," Mark answered. "I think she wants to show you her ring."

"Then I think you and Judy should go out to dinner. Leave the old folks behind. Have a romantic night out. I know just the place and I can get you a good table. Will you trust me for that?"

"Thanks, Don," Mark said.

The Aragon Restaurant had a Spanish motif. Servers wore black, flat, wide-brimmed hats. Hand-painted clay pots stood like sentries in each corner and at each side of the main entrance into the dining room. The Aragon was perfect for what Mark had in mind. He patted his coat pocket for the third time to make sure the rings were there. Judy dressed for the event. It was still cool in June, so Judy wore a light sweater over a white silk blouse and a short skirt.

Mark picked up the scent of White Shoulders as he sat across from her trying to find the right moment to pop the question. Never had he seen servers so efficient. Whenever he was ready to go for it, he was interrupted. After ordering dessert, Mark told the server that they were going to step outside on the veranda and would return to their table in a few minutes. He took Judy by the hand through doors already opened to a porch that over-looked several acres of wooded land. The night sky was clear. Mark put his coat around Judy and they sat on an ornate concrete bench surrounded by flowering vines. Holding her hand he lowered himself to one knee. "Judy Archer, will you marry me?" he asked in a quiet but steady voice.

"Nothing would make me happier," she said. Mark stood and lifted Judy to her feet. He reached around her to get the rings from his coat pocket, and they froze in a tight embrace. Nothing was said. Under the stars, they stood in perfect unity. Judy broke the silence. "Are you going to give me a ring?" she teased. Mark opened the small box, removed the engagement ring, and then placed it on Judy's finger. She gazed at the ring, then looked up into Mark's face. "I have never loved any man as much as I love you, Mark. I want nothing more than to grow old with you." If Mark could only know, Judy thought, how much she wanted that.

When the evening ended, Mark slept on a sofa/sleeper in the den, and Judy went to her room on the second floor. As she passed by her parents' room she tapped quietly on the door, knowing that her mother would be awake. In a moment, her mother slipped out of the door into the hallway dressed in her nightgown. "Well, did something wonderful happen to-night?" she asked with a smile, reaching for Judy's hand. Judy showed her the engagement ring and gave a brief whispered account of the evening.

"I'm so happy for you, Judy. I know that things will work out for you, honey. Don can't stop talking about Mark." Just as his name was men-tioned, Don Douglas stumbled into the hallway in his pajamas, his hair tousled and eyes half-closed.

"Well, do we have good news?" he asked.

"He proposed, Dad, but I know that you already know that. Thanks for making him feel so welcome." Don wrapped his arms around the two women in his life, and the three of them stood in perfect family harmony.

Don broke the reverie. "It's time to go to bed. Tomorrow we'll cel-ebrate." Judy went to her room. Sleep came quickly.

• • •

Judy had packed the wedding planner, so on their return flight they began to discuss the particulars of the event. It was already decided that the wedding would be "practical." Only family and close friends from the police department and the high school would be invited. Pastor Dressler would officiate, and the honeymoon would be in New Hampshire at the Garrison chalet.

The Garrison chalet, as it was called, was a chalet-style vacation home situated near the White Mountains in Woodsville, New Hampshire. It had belonged to Mark's grandparents, then to his parents, and now to him.

When the plane completed its taxi to the gate, passengers began to stand and remove their carry-on luggage from the overhead compartments. As Judy took a step into the aisle, she fell backwards into the arms of the passenger behind her. Recovering, she apologized and continued to gather her luggage. With passengers crowded in the aisle, Mark hadn't been able to get out of his seat to help her. After they departed from the plane and were in the terminal, Mark asked what had happened. "I tripped, I guess," Judy said. "It was very embarrassing."

4

While Mark and Judy were at her parents, George received another call, this time on his mobile phone. He fumbled with the phone as he drove, trying to find the button with the telephone icon, all the time saying, "Hello." Finally, he heard a response.

"Are you driving, George?" the caller asked without a greeting.

"Yes," he replied. "How did you get this number?"

"I have my ways. Pull over. I don't want you to have an accident. It wouldn't be good for either of us." George pulled to the shoulder of the road. "Are you ready to deal?" the caller asked.

"I've been instructed by my management to secure the disks," he said.

"Good, does your management know the price?" the caller asked, putting a cynical emphasis on the word "management."

"They know the asking price, but they're not willing to pay it," George answered.

"My finger is on the format button, George. It's up to you."

"We're willing to meet you halfway. Another $50,000 for the text disks. That's all that I can offer," George said, knowing that Bio-Gen would pay twice the asking price for the disks, if necessary.

"$75,000, Georgie boy, and you have five seconds before I format these disks," the caller said. The counting began, "one…two…three…"

"When and where can I have them, and how do I know that you won't copy them?" George interrupted.

"Smart move. I'll work out the transfer and get back to you, George. And you don't." The caller hung up.

• • •

"We missed the donuts," Sue said to Mark as he returned to the Riverside police station with a box of Dunkin' Donuts under his arm. He had been the "donut man" on the RPD for many years.

"Don't tell me you ate fruit or something healthy," he quipped.

"Nope, we had donut DT's," she replied.

Mark dropped the donuts on the break table in the squad room and headed for his desk. His work consisted of overseeing the officers, and taking charge of investigations in the field. Sue reported to Lieutenant Corcoran. After Mark was settled in to his routine for several hours, the phone on his desk rang. It was Ed Braun. "Did you get my message?" Ed asked.

"What message?" Mark asked.

"I left a message yesterday that you should call me when you got back," Ed replied.

"No message, Ed. It must have gotten misplaced," Mark said with a concern in his voice. There was a message board in the squad room. Mark turned to face the message board and saw nothing under his name. Lost messages could be lost opportunities. "I apologize. What's up?"

"I just wanted you to know that I spoke with the cleanup crew leader," Ed said. "Are you going to have lunch at Marge's today? I could meet you there."

"How about 11:30, Ed?"

"See you there," Ed said as he hung up the phone.

On the way out of the office, Mark asked Sue whether she had taken a message from Ed. "Sure, I put it on the board," she replied. She had no explanation for its absence.

Ed wasn't there when Mark arrived, so he ordered lunch at the counter and saved the empty stool next to him. Marge set up two places and filled two water glasses. "What about lunch, Mark? Want to order or are you going to wait for Ed?"

"You know the drill, Marge. Let's order." She handed Cookie an order for the Monday special—fried calf's liver with onions, and mashed potatoes. At the same moment, Ed slipped onto the stool next to Mark.

"Make it two," Ed said to Marge. He turned to Mark. "You'd better shape up your troops, Mark."

"Explain," Mark said.

"I'm glad my call yesterday wasn't a 911 call, or I'd be dead," Ed said.

"I spoke to Sue about that, Ed. I don't think it'll happen again. We're pretty careful about messages." Not wanting to pursue the missed message, Mark asked, "What did you find out from the crew leader?"

"He remembered the event. He was called the next day about the missing box. All he could say was what he had already said—that the box was on your desk at the station, and the technician took it outside to the dumpster with the rest of the trash."

"Why would they have done that, Ed? It seems unusual to me that a cleaning crew would take something from the top of a desk, especially when it was clearly not trash."

"Well, that's not exactly the case," Ed responded. "There was a note on the box."

"What note?" Mark asked.

"There was one of those little yellow stick-on notes with the word 'trash' stuck to the box. The crew leader removed it and placed the box next to the waste containers for removal. The technician then took it outside when she cleaned the room."

Mark was puzzled. When Sue called the crew members on the day following the disappearance of the box she reported that the technician had removed the box from the top of the desk, and that it was unmarked. He would need to clear this up. No one would have any reason to tag the box as trash.

School was out, and Mark's schedule was light, so Mark and Judy decided to meet at the municipal park in Riverside to talk about the wedding. Judy pulled paper and pen from her bag, along with two bottles of water. She handed a water bottle to Mark and wrote "Guests" at the top of a sheet of paper. "Here comes the hard part, Mark," she said. "We have to decide how many and who to invite to our 'practical' wedding."

"How about just inviting Pastor Dressler?" Mark said, half-kidding.

"Is this going to be difficult?" Judy asked as she brought Mark's face to hers and kissed him lightly.

"Okay. How many should we invite?"

It didn't take long for them to list the relatives. Friends were another matter. Judy had friends from high school, college, the school where she taught, and the church. Mark had a few from the police station and Riverside. It began to look as though the bride's side would be SRO, while the groom's side would be in the front pew.

Planning the guest list was a revelation for Judy. Mark had not shared much about himself. He had met her family, napped in the bedroom she had grown up in, and met some of her friends at church, but she realized that he had shared very little about himself. Judy knew that his parents were dead and that he was an only child. What about aunts and uncles? Army friends? High school friends? All she knew about his background was that he had been in love in the sixth grade. She went to her Escort and got a heavy wool blanket from the trunk. Returning, she spread the blanket on the ground next to the picnic bench. Mark lay on the blanket, and Judy lay on her side perpendicular to Mark with her head on his stomach. Mark pulled his Cubs cap over his eyes. "Tell me about yourself, Mark," Judy said. "I mean about your friends."

It was difficult for Mark. Much of his growing up years were a blur. He had been a loner, not consciously ashamed of his parents but living the lie that troubled families live. Bring no one home. Lose the invitations to parent/teacher conferences. Make up stories when school starts in the Fall and everyone tells about their family vacations. Mark had always been an athlete, but he competed mainly against himself or the clock, preferring individual sports to team sports. That way he couldn't disappoint anyone but himself. It was in the Army that he began his journey toward self-discovery, but it wasn't until he met Dr. Lum that he learned what normal was. How much should he tell Judy?

"I haven't done a very good job of keeping track of my friends, Judy," he admitted. In fact, he could list his close friends on a matchbook. "Jeff, Corky, Ed Braun, Marge, and you are about it for now," he confessed. Judy said nothing. She scooted herself toward Mark's face, removed his cap, and kissed him gently, then lay alongside him quietly. Mark's throat was dry, and his eyes were getting moist. Frozen feelings were beginning to melt.

• • •

At the end of June, Judy and Mark drove to the Skokie Courthouse to apply for a marriage license. A middle-aged lady came to the counter, "May I help you," she asked.

"We'd like to apply for a marriage license," Judy answered.

"I need identification showing your birth dates," the clerk said. Judy slid the manila folder holding her documents across the counter. Mark removed his driver's license from his wallet.

"Do you have a driver's license with a picture?" the lady asked Judy.

"Yes," Judy answered, reaching for her purse.

The lady handed Judy's documents and the manila folder to Mark while Judy removed her driver's license from her wallet. While placing Judy's birth certificate in the manila folder, Mark glanced at the document and was surprised to see that it listed as her biological parents, Lois (Snyder) Hammond, mother, and Richard Hammond, father. He began to ask her who these people were when the clerk slid a form across the counter for them to sign. While Judy was signing, the clerk asked Mark for thirty dollars in cash. Mark paid the fee, then signed above his typed name. After a brief wait, they were handed a three-part license which they were instructed to give to the officiating minister or public official. Thanking the clerk, they left.

On the way out of the building, Mark asked, "Who are the Hammond's?"

Ignoring his question, Judy said, "Mark, I need to use the ladies room before we head back. Will you wait here for a moment?" She was furious at herself for bringing the birth certificate and needed time to think about what she would tell Mark. She knew he wouldn't let it go.

As Judy approached Mark in the hallway outside of the ladies room, he asked again, "Judy, who are the Hammond's?"

"Richard Hammond is my biological father. He died when I was eleven. My mother then married Don Douglas. I thought that I had mentioned that Don was my stepfather."

"I think I would have remembered that," Mark said, puzzled. "How did your father die?"

"I'd rather not discuss it now, Mark," Judy said with finality, and began to walk toward the elevator. Mark let it drop, for the time being.

• • •

George had never met his blackmailer. Their conversations had been on the phone. The first transfer of money had taken place in Hollywood style—he left the money as instructed in a paper sack at a designated place in a small neighborhood park near Bio-Gen. The Executive Committee of Bio-Gen left the details to George. They were between a rock and a hard place. Because Dr. Archer had jeopardized the company's credibility, they couldn't go to the police and gamble on a scandal that could endanger their contract with NIH. Instead, they would have to play along until they had the disks and were able to review his work. George wondered when he would receive instructions for the next transaction. He didn't have long to wait.

After hanging his sport coat on a coat rack in the corner of his office, George turned toward his desk then noticed an envelope in the lower right pocket of his coat. He didn't recall putting it there. The envelope was unmarked and sealed. Inside was a piece of paper torn from a bound pad with the words "Things to do Today" printed at the top. A short message was handwritten, "Leave your package at 4:00 P.M. at the Austin Avenue YMCA, lobby locker forty-two."

How had the envelope gotten into his coat pocket? It was not there when he dressed in the morning, and he had driven directly to Bio-Gen. The only place that he had been close to anyone was in the elevator. The elevator wasn't crowded, but he was preoccupied and hadn't paid attention to who was behind him. The note was the first tangible piece of evidence that might identify the blackmailer. George understood Bio-Gen's need to keep the matter under cover, but he wished that he could get help from a law enforcement agency. He would have to meet with his management quickly if he were to have $75,000 in cash before the afternoon. He set up a mid-morning meeting with Rory Sanders, Chief Operating Officer of Bio-Gen, and Keith Lawson, Chief Financial Officer.

Rory Sanders, a large man of six feet, two inches and 190 pounds, had the appearance of a former athlete; however, during the latter of his forty-eight years he had developed a pear-shaped paunch, a tailor's nightmare. His head was mismatched with eyes too small for his round face and football neck. Gray was mixed with black in what was left of his hair. With a booming bass voice, the dream of any choir director, he seemed unable to whisper.

Keith Lawson was the opposite of Rory Sanders. A Harvard MBA with a flawless track record in the industry, Lawson had brought financial integrity to Bio-Gen by negotiating the contract with NIH that assured Bio-Gen's participation in the Human Genome Project. Lawson was small, five feet, seven inches, weighing 155 pounds, in excellent physical condition—a man who could buy fashionable suits off of the rack. Years of pouring over numbers had dimmed his vision, requiring thick tri-focals, but he was handsome nevertheless, and had a winning personality. Most important for his position, his word was his bond. Sanders ordered Lawson to give George the $75,000.

George had never been to the Austin Avenue YMCA on the northwest side of Chicago. Entering the tile lobby, George looked straight ahead at the reception desk. To the left of the desk was a turnstile entranceway separating the cardholding members from the trespassers. He approached the reception desk and asked directions to the lobby lockers. The teenager attending the desk pointed George to a large lobby area between the main entrance and the reception desk.

Walking through the empty sitting room, George found a door with the sign "public lockers." Inside was what had once been a cloakroom. The walls were lined with small lockers, originally used for hats, gloves, and umbrellas of guests attending concerts, lectures, or worship services in the Y assembly hall. Finding locker forty-two, he removed an envelope from the inner pocket of his sport coat and a quarter from his pants pocket. He placed the envelope in locker forty-two, put the quarter in the slot, and locked the door. Removing the key, he placed it in his pocket, wondering how the caller would remove the contents from the locker, and how long the Y would allow the locker to be rented before they opened it. His curiosity was soon satisfied.

As he approached his car George swore under his breath, wondering what he had done to deserve a parking ticket. The white envelope tucked under his windshield wiper was unmarked. Inside was another note written on paper torn from the same pad as the note that had been slipped into his sport coat that morning. This one read, "Place the key in this envelope and leave it in the emergency telephone box in the elevator at the Austin Avenue public parking garage three blocks north of the Y. Your disks are there. If you fail to leave the key, the remaining eighteen disks will be formatted. I will watch until your car is gone. Do this before 4:30 P.M." George looked at his watch. It was just 4:00.

The parking garage was crowded with commuters heading home. He had no trouble finding a place to park on the second level. At 4:15 he approached the elevator and pushed the down button. The sign above the elevator doors showed that it was on the sixth level. At the second floor three people entered with George and continued to the ground level where all departed. George immediately pushed the button to close the doors and midway between the first and second level he pushed the red emergency stop. Opening the emergency telephone box, he found a white envelope containing four disks. He replaced it with the envelope containing the locker key, released the emergency stop, and then proceeded to the second level. He departed the elevator and drove to his office at Bio-Gen.

Pastor Dressler greeted Mark and Judy at the entrance to the Pastor's office on the side of the church building. After declining his offer of coffee, Mark and Judy sat in the two chairs in front of Dressler's desk. Dressler went through his standard opening remarks and gathered personal information for the church records. Then he asked about the time, date, and place for the rehearsal, wedding, and reception. After the fact gathering, he asked, "What kind of wedding do you have in mind—traditional or contemporary?"

"I'll yield to Judy," Mark said.

Both looked at Judy, but she didn't reply. She was gazing at Mark without expression. Mark said, "Judy, it's up to you."

Judy continued to look at Mark, then said, "What?"

Mark glanced at Pastor Dressler. He was looking at Judy but said nothing. Mark spoke again to Judy, "Pastor asked whether we want a traditional or contemporary wedding."

"Traditional," she said.

After the meeting, as Mark drove Judy home in his police vehicle, he asked, "Judy, are you okay?"

"What do you mean, Mark?"

"At one point during our meeting you seemed to lose concentration."

"I must have been day-dreaming," Judy said, dismissing Mark's question. She didn't know how to describe what had happened. For a moment she seemed to have lost focus. This had never happened before.

Judy spent the month of July making final arrangements for the wedding. By the middle of August, forty-one guests had responded favorably, including all of the people Mark invited and most of Judy's guests.

After the wedding rehearsal, there was an air of anticipation. Mark, Corky, and Jeff left from the church for their "boys' night out." Judy and her parents then headed to Becky Malott's apartment. Becky was Judy's best friend, colleague, and maid of honor. Mark and Judy would not see each other again until the wedding at 10:00 A.M. the following day.

The "boys' night out" was everything Mark had hoped for—low key. He had made it known that he did not want any surprises. Corky and Jeff took him to a club in the city where they had "monster" prime ribs followed by some drinks. A small group played dinner music.

Mark got home by 11:00 P.M. and went to sleep at once.

After dessert at Becky's, Judy and her parents returned to her townhouse where Don Douglas went to bed. Lois and Judy drank Chamomile tea in the living room. "This is the room where I met Mark. He came to tell me that Bob's body had been found in the Des Plaines River. It was a day that I'll never forget, and I still remember how gentle Mark was in his own way. Without asking, I hugged him. He held me for the longest time, and I could just feel his strength. Somehow I knew that there was something special about him."

"Have you discussed your father with him yet, Judy?" Lois asked.

"I can't bring myself to do it," she replied.

"Is that fair, Judy?" Lois inquired.

"No, it isn't, but I'm getting to the age where my chances are better, aren't I?"

"They say that each year after forty your chances of getting sick get less, but there are exceptions. There are no guarantees, Judy. Only a test will tell for sure before the symptoms begin. Have you had any symptoms?"

"I don't think so. At the Pastor's office I blanked out for a minute. I don't know what that was all about. Is that a symptom? Did Daddy do that?" She was referring to Richard Hammond.

"Yes, he did. They called them seizures. Some just lasted a few seconds. Some lasted a few minutes. Did you call the doctor?" Lois asked.

"No, of course not. It was just for a second. I have been a little stressed with the whole situation, Mom. Could you tell me how it was with Daddy?"

Lois was startled. In the past, when Richard's name was mentioned, Judy covered her ears or left the room. She worked hard to forget the torment of his disease and the turmoil it caused in the family during her young life. "Are you sure you want to do this, Judy?" Lois asked. Judy nodded. Lois got a throw pillow and sat on the floor at Judy's feet, leaning her head on Judy's knee. She sat silently for awhile, then began to talk.

"Richard Hammond was the first man I ever truly loved," she began. "He was smart, athletic, and full of life. He swept me off of my feet." Judy was stunned. She had never known that side of her biological father.

"When did he get sick?" Judy asked.

"After we had been married a year or so he started having symptoms. You had just been born and weren't sleeping well at night. I thought that his behavior was due to lack of sleep. He was also working long hours. It was nothing terribly obvious—he staggered slightly, but just occasionally. He became forgetful, and he developed a slight twitch in his hands. I didn't pay much attention to those things, but what really concerned me was his attitude. Richard was the kindest man you could ever meet. He would never speak ill of anyone, and he treated me like a queen. But when the symptoms started he became impatient and critical. That was when I knew that something was wrong."

"Didn't he have sickness in his family?"

"Two of his father's brothers died of Huntington's, but there was little information about the disease then. We had no reason to think that it was hereditary; otherwise, we'd have made different choices."

"Meaning me?" Judy asked.

"Possibly," her mother answered honestly. "It would have been a wrong choice, Judy. You are the best thing that happened from our marriage, although I wouldn't take anything for that first year with Richard."

The two sat silently together occasionally sipping their tea. Her mother had never stopped loving Richard Hammond while he was alive, and refused outside care for the first several years of his sickness. She fed him, bathed him, and changed his diapers during the final years of his life, taking constant verbal abuse. She spoke softly to him, remembering the man he once had been. At 1:00 A.M. the two went to their rooms. Judy lay awake for a long time uneasy about withholding the truth from Mark. Lois went to sleep at once cuddled in Donald's arms.

5

No one set an alarm for the wedding day. Donald was the first one in Judy's townhouse to awaken. He glanced at the clock. It was 7:30 A.M., only two and one half hours until the wedding! He shook Lois, then went to Judy's room and tapped on the door. He heard her stir, then tapped again. This time he said, "Judy, it's 7:30." He heard a groan, then the sound of feet hitting the floor.

"Thanks, Dad," she said through the door in a sleepy voice.

The house came alive to the sounds of showers and shavers. Donald made breakfast for the three of them, then ate while the women primped. Judy was the first to get to the kitchen. She was in her slip and slippers. "Thanks for getting me up, Dad," she said as she slid into a chair at the kitchen table and organized her food.

"Is Mom about ready?" Richard asked, but before Judy could answer Lois entered the kitchen and sat across from Judy. She reached across the table and took Judy's hand.

"Judy, may I have a prayer before we eat?" Lois asked. "And will you join us, Donald?"

The three held hands while Lois prayed. Her prayer was spontaneous, asking God to be a full partner with Mark and Judy in their marriage, and asking that Judy be spared the sickness that had taken her father. She also thanked God for Judy and for all that she meant to her and Donald. They squeezed hands and continued with their breakfast.

Mark arrived early at the church. Jeff was waiting in his car in front of the church and got out when Mark pulled up. "I brought you something, Mark. Do you want it now?"

"You didn't need to do that, Jeff," Mark said, extending his hand to receive the small package from Jeff. Mark opened the box and found a piece of paper folded over four times. Unfolding the paper, he could see that it was a letter under the RPD letterhead. Jeff's name was on the bottom. It was formally addressed to Sergeant Mark Garrison. The letter read, "Dear Sergeant Garrison, It gives me great pleasure to inform you that you have passed the qualifications necessary to be advanced to the rank of lieutenant in the Riverside Police Department. At the next annual recognition banquet you will receive your new insignia; however, your advancement will be effective immediately. You will be in charge of a new investigation section of the RPD. Congratulations, Captain Jeffrey A. Myers."

"How can this be?" Mark asked Jeff. "I just took the final exam last week."

"The exam was only part of our consideration, Mark. The Police Board was pleased with the results of the exam but more pleased with your performance. This will mean organizing a special investigations unit, Mark. As you know, Riverside is growing and we will be adding two additional officers during the coming year. One of them will be trained to work with you."

Mark pumped Jeff's hand, having a slight inclination to give him a hug, but frozen feelings hadn't melted down to that degree. In time. As the two were turning toward the church, Lieutenant Corcoran, now Mark's equal in rank, joined them. He was already aware of the promotion, but waited until something was said. Jeff spoke next, "Corky, meet the newest lieutenant in the Riverside Police Department."

"All I can say, Mark," said Corky, "is that you deserve it, but remember who the best man is at this wedding!" They all laughed.

At 9:50 A.M. the guests were seated, the groom and his best man were in their assigned position, and the organist began to play. Becky Malott walked slowly down the aisle to the sounds of The Wedding March, followed by Judy on the arm of her father. Mark had never seen Judy look more beautiful. Her tea-length dress, her bouquet, and the glow on her face unfroze more feelings in him than anything ever had. He fought hard not to cry, then decided that it was okay. The tears flowed down his cheeks. Donald Douglas, too, cried unashamedly as he answered the Pastor's question on behalf of Lois and himself, "Who gives this woman to this man?"

Donald answered, "Her mother and I do," then took his place along-side Lois as Mark and Judy advanced to their positions in front of the Pastor. The words of the service were spoken without fault, no one fainted, and the attendants presented the rings at the right time. Pastor Dressler spoke a brief homily based on the second chapter of Genesis.

The recessional was lively after which the wedding party and guests moved at once to the Fellowship Hall. When the guests were in the room, Corky announced the arrival of "Lieutenant and Mrs. Mark Garrison." The guests clapped and the newly married couple made their way through the crowd receiving congratulations and hugs.

Judy whispered in Mark's ear as they stood waiting for the cake cutting, "Did Corky say Lieutenant and Mrs. Garrison?" putting the emphasis on the rank.

"That's what he said," Mark replied with a smile. "Jeff's wedding present to us was a letter of promotion."

"Congratulations, Lieutenant," Judy said, as she kissed him to the applause of the guests.

"I have the narrative disks," George said as he sat down in the office of the Chief Executive Officer of Bio-Gen, Aaron Krimer III. Krimer was a fit man of five feet, ten inches, and 165 pounds. At fifty-eight his hair was suspiciously jet-black and coifed like a Baptist preacher. Impeccably dressed, he wore a gray Joseph Abboud three-button suit made of wool crepe. Shirt, tie, and belt were carefully chosen to match the thin cream-colored stripe in his suit. Black, hand-made Bespoke Status Shoes added several inches to his height without telling the secret. Krimer's face was triangular with delicate features. While broad, his forehead was short. Dark eyes looked directly at George Palmer as he placed a small package on the desk in front of the CEO.

"Have you read them?" Krimer asked.

"Not yet," George replied. "I picked them up today."

"How long will it take to read four ZIP disks?" the CEO asked.

"Probably several days," George answered.

"Bring Michele Phillips up to speed on this, George, and the two of you read the disks and report back to me. Only the Executive Committee, you, and Michele are to be part of this, George. Is that acceptable to you?"

"At this point it is, sir," George answered.

"Set aside your other work for now, George, and put this at the top of your priority list," Krimer said as he rose and walked to the door, signalling that the meeting was over. "And by the way, George, this time make a copy of the disks and keep them in a safe place." George understood the rebuke.

The Executive Committee, consisting of Krimer, Chief Executive Officer, Rory Sanders, and Keith Lawson, was aware that Bob Archer had reported directly to George. The clandestine work done by Archer was done on George's watch. George had also allowed Archer's associate, Dr. Bev Hudson, to analyze Archer's work at home, a direct violation of company policy. It was there that the original disks were stolen during a burglary and subsequently destroyed. George had instructed Dr. Hudson to prepare a duplicate set of disks, but was told at the time of the burglary that none had been made. Only afterward when he received a call from the blackmailer did he learn that there was a duplicate set of disks. George had lost control of the Archer affair and it had cost the lives of doctors Archer and Hudson, risked the future of Bio-Gen, and jeopardized his own career. He headed at once for the office of Dr. Michele Phillips.

Dr. Phillips had taken over Project 314 after Bob Archer's suicide. The project was back on track thanks to her superb skills and commitment. She was excited to be part of the Human Genome Project, especially being the youngest scientist at Bio-Gen. At twenty-eight, Dr. Phillips had established herself as a geneticist of great promise.

George seldom visited Michele now that she had established herself at Bio-Gen. They had a good relationship and mutual respect. "How are you, Dr. Phillips?" he asked after tapping on the door of the small office adjacent to her lab.

"Just getting ready to head for home," Michele answered.

"Do you have thirty minutes?" George asked.

"Certainly," Michele answered, mentally canceling her plans for an evening bike ride on a nearby trail.

When George spoke he was clear and concise. It didn't take him long to review the history of the Archer episode. Michele already knew some of the story. Archer's indiscretion at work and subsequent suicide had been gossip fare since the scandal, but nothing was known of his work on Gene 15105, the whole matter having been kept a well-guarded secret. When George explained that company management had asked him to partner with her in reading the four ZIP disks containing the narrative description of Archer's work, she quickly agreed. Her love for mystery and suspense and her curious scientific mind made her the logical candidate for this assignment. Once again, the work on Project 314 would be delayed, but it was hoped that the narration on the disks could be summarized, reported, and quickly retired to file within several weeks. In fact, this would be the beginning of a new chapter.

George and Michele were in the fourth day of reading the narrative disks. Both were stunned by what Bob Archer had done. Along with many in the scientific community, George had great respect for Dr. Archer. Bio-Gen had considered him their rising star. When Bob discovered a common mutation in Gene 15105 of the Human Genome DNA samples being studied, he was astounded. A mutation by definition is a unique alteration. He confirmed the universality of the mutation by surreptitiously gaining access to the DNA samples of Bio-Gen employees, the first of his many offenses.

Bob then set aside his assigned work on Project 314 to find a repair for the mutation. In this way, he expected to discover what role Gene 15105 plays in the human condition. Abandoning his assigned work was his second offense.

Amazingly, Bob discovered a remedy for the mutation within months, as well as a means for introducing the remedy into the human body. Michele and George were just reading the narrative disk in which Bob described his first attempt at treating a living human. "How could he have proceeded with human trials without approval?" Michele asked George. She was thoroughly familiar with scientific protocol.

"This first trial was done on a man who was housed on death row at Riverside Correctional Institute, a man called Harley," George said. "Apparently Bob felt that since the man was sentenced to die, the risk was tolerable."

"No one has that right," Michele stated with conviction.

"Let's see what happened with Harley," George said, returning to his monitor. Appalled that Bob had arranged to smuggle the remedy into the prison, they were equally amazed that the prisoner had agreed to participate in the experiment. Harley was, apparently, a rebel without a cause. Nevertheless, the remedy caused amazing results in a short period of time. Gene 15105 seemed to govern Harley's overall physical, mental, and spiritual health. Under treatment, Harley improved in all these areas, overcoming a heart condition, a sociopathic personality, and a spiritual vacuum.

"This is amazing," Michele Phillips said. "The prisoner did a complete turnaround. What has happened to him since Dr. Archer died?"

"I don't know," George answered, "but we can find out. I'll call a man I know at the Riverside Police Department, a Sergeant Mark Garrison. He was involved in the investigation of Dr. Archer and Dr. Hudson's deaths. Now, let's call it a day. We'll continue reading the disks tomorrow."

George left Michele's office and proceeded to his own. He got the telephone number of the Riverside Police Department from the operator, then placed the call. The voice that answered the phone sounded familiar to George, but he wasn't sure why. He was told that Sergeant Garrison was now Lieutenant Garrison, and that he was on his honeymoon and wouldn't be back until the following week. George left his number and asked that Lieutenant Garrison return his call at the earliest possible time. Immediately, George realized the mistake that he had made. He was under instructions to keep the Archer issue in house. Garrison would know immediately that he had the disks if he mentioned the name Harley. He would have to make his inquiry about Harley without Garrison and cover his tracks as best he could.

On the following day, George and Michele read the fourth and final disk. This disk was a narration of another human trial, this time on a young woman in Virginia. On the disk Bob noted how he had met the woman, and why she was selected as a candidate for his experiment. She was HIV-positive and had active AIDS. "She, too, was waiting to die," George noted as he and Michele read with growing astonishment.

"But why would she agree to this?" Michele puzzled, more to herself than to George.

"Why do cancer patients go to Mexico to take alternative treatments?" George answered. "When someone is under a death sentence what is the real risk?"

This second person, Barbara Arnold, amazingly experienced complete remission from AIDS and, like Harley, experienced general improvement. Bob had discovered the effect of Gene 15105 on the human body. It was the gene that governed overall wellbeing.

"What became of Barbara Arnold?" Michele asked.

"I am trying to find out what became of Harley," George answered. "Why don't you do some checking on Barbara Arnold, then let's compare notes. Let me know the minute you find out anything."

Michele re-read the narrative portion covering the personal data on Barbara Arnold and called her telephone number in Richmond, Virginia. A man answered, "Hello."

"Hello," replied Michele. "May I speak with Barbara Arnold, please?"

"This is Barbara's brother. Who's calling?" he asked.

"My name is Dr. Michele Phillips. I'm with Bio-Gen Laboratories and I'm following up on work done by Dr. Bob Archer. It's important that I speak with Barbara Arnold."

"I'm sorry, Dr. Phillips, but you're too late. Barbara died shortly after the death of Dr. Archer. She wasn't able to get the medicine she needed."

"I'm very sorry," Michele offered, "thank you." She hung up and called George.

"Barbara Arnold died. Apparently the remedy that Dr. Archer provided did not alter 15105 permanently. When Dr. Archer died and there was no further treatment, she reverted to her former condition."

"If Barbara Arnold died, Harley is also dead," George said. "The prison should have no reason not to confirm that. Call Riverside Correctional Institute and see if you can verify the death of a prisoner known as Harley."

Michele was connected to the public information office at RCI. They acknowledged that the prisoner known as Harley had indeed died of heart failure while housed at the prison, but they could not reveal more than that. It was all that Michele needed to know.

The two scientists met with the Executive Committee of Bio-Gen and shared their findings from the narrative disks. Agreement was reached quickly on the need to acquire the eighteen data disks still in the hands of the blackmailer.

Aaron Krimer III, quick to see an opportunity, said, "We all know the risk that public disclosure of Dr. Archer's work poses for Bio-Gen. On the other hand, Dr. Archer's work, although unethically conducted, opens possibilities for significant discovery. George, it is essential that you get the remaining disks. In the meantime, the Executive Committee will decide whether we should continue what Dr. Archer began, but in a way that meets accepted protocol."

"The initiative for acquiring the remaining disks," said George, "is in the hands of the blackmailer. I have no way of knowing who this person is, or how to make contact."

"Rest assured, George," said the CEO, "contact will be made. There is much at stake here for everyone, including the blackmailer."

George and Michele resumed their usual activities, waiting for the blackmailer to take the next step. Again, George wouldn't have long to wait.

Judy had never been to New England. August wasn't the best month to visit. In four to six weeks, the trees would begin to change and the scenery would be glorious, but to compensate for missing the colors, Mark planned a busy week of sightseeing and relaxing. He was eager to visit the New Hampshire chalet once again.

Mark turned off of the crushed stone road onto a small gravel parking area in front of the chalet. The building sat on one and one-half acres, mostly wooded. It was surrounded by approximately 100 feet of spotty lawn that barely survived on occasional gifts of sunlight through the pine trees. The walk from the stone parking area to the chalet was approximately seventy-five feet, mostly uphill. Judy was thrilled with the chalet. Since the property had been in the family for a long time, she envisioned something entirely different. "This isn't what I expected," she said to Mark as he took her on a walking tour around the property.

"In the Seventies we replaced the old building with what you see. The owners in this area pooled their money and built a small ski slope, then dammed a creek to make a small fishing and swimming lake. We formed an organization to maintain the facilities. Covenants were written to require each owner to meet certain standards, so some of us with older buildings had to decide whether to sell or update. My grandfather loved this site, as did my father. I came here as a boy and had many adventures in these woods. It was not a hard decision to update."

The chalet was built to resemble Swiss chalets. A simple a-frame building, the right front exterior was made of vertical wood siding painted in a plum color. One window on that side sat above a large flower box well tended. The left front exterior was white stucco with wood trim in a Tudor style. Doors and windows were of modern aluminum triple-track construction. All the sides were plum-colored vertical wood siding. Judy could see that the property was well cared for.

A wooden freestanding storage shed stood at the rear of the property. As they approached the shed, a black snake slithered from under the shed and disappeared in the brush at the edge of the woods. Judy yelped, then retreated several steps. Mark laughed although he, too, took a step in retreat. "Are there lots of snakes here?" Judy asked, ready to return to her townhouse.

"Not really, Judy," Mark answered. "You'll always find them around this wood shed."

"No," Judy said firmly. "You will always find them around this wood shed, because I don't ever intend to come near here."

"Do you ski, Judy?" Mark asked.

"Never."

"Would you like to try?"

"On a beginner's slope?"

"Of course," Mark answered. She agreed, and Mark was delighted. They walked around the chalet and returned to the car to begin unpacking. Judy carried her guitar and a hanging bag, while Mark picked up two suitcases. When they got to the front door, Mark set everything down and lifted his new bride over the threshold. While she was still in his arms, she kissed him. He put her down and they embraced for a long time.

The inside of the chalet held more surprises. Judy had seen the brick chimney on the outside, but she had no idea that the fireplace was the center of attention. Walking into the house from the front door, the fireplace was on the right embedded in a floor to ceiling brick wall. A cast-iron insert returned heat from the fire into the room. There were four rooms in the chalet—a main living area which included the living room, kitchen, and eating alcove, a screened-in porch, and, rising several steps, a hallway leading to a bedroom on the right and another on the left, with a shared bathroom in-between. The entire interior was wood paneled. Drapery and curtains were sadly in need of replacement. "These curtains have to go," Judy remarked as they toured the upper level.

"I've never seen them before," Mark said. "The tenants must have hung them. We'll replace them when their contract ends."

The chalet was clean and it was obvious that the present tenants were taking care of the place. Mark was pleased and happy that Judy liked the house. The refrigerator was mostly empty, so after they unpacked Judy made a shopping list while Mark made a careful inspection of the interior of the chalet.

There wasn't time for a tour of Woodsville, so Mark took Judy to AG Supermarkets to shop for groceries. He added some light bulbs to her cart, and then they took their place in line at the check-out counter. As Judy placed the items on the counter she removed the light bulbs from the cart, then swung around toward Mark. "I didn't put these in the cart," she said angrily. "What are they doing here?"

Mark was shocked. Judy's eyes were opened wide and she was glaring at him. The young girl behind the counter was embarrassed and looked away. "Some of the bulbs were burned out at the chalet," he said calmly. "I didn't find any bulbs in the cabinets, so I put them in your cart."

"The least you could have done was tell me," Judy said sternly.

Mark didn't know how to react. He had never seen this side of Judy. She was obviously angry, but over light bulbs? It didn't make sense. He paid the bill and they left the supermarket returning to the car. When they were seated Mark spoke first. "That was a bit of a scene in there."

"Mark, I don't know what to say. I don't know what came over me. I am so sorry."

"I think that we are both tired," Mark offered. "Maybe it would be good for us to fix dinner and get some rest. We can plan the rest of our vacation in the morning."

"That's fine," Judy agreed. She was ashamed of what had happened, but more afraid of its sudden onset. The anger had come from nowhere. In one moment she was happy just to be near Mark. In the next moment she was a vixen. Why? What had overtaken her?

At the same time Mark was assessing the outburst. He had offered a quick and easy excuse, but he knew that they weren't tired, having gotten plenty of rest during their trip. There was something at work here, something that confounded Judy at that moment. He wouldn't say anything further, letting Judy raise the subject if she chose.

Too many unexplainable things have happened recently, Judy thought as they drove quietly to the chalet. The fall in the airplane, blacking out in the Pastor's office, and now this. She decided that she would call her mother the first time that Mark was away from the chalet.

After returning from a day trip to the top of Mt. Washington, Mark fell asleep in a chaise lounge in the screened-in porch. Judy walked down to the lake, about one quarter mile from the chalet. The small lake was at the bottom of a sloping hill, accessible by stone steps. It offered a short sand beach for wading and, on the opposite side, a fifteen-foot pier for fishing. Sitting in the shade of a gazebo near the sand beach, she removed her mobile phone from her fanny-pack and dialed her mother's number.

Lois answered. Judy could hear the sound of kitchenware or dishes in the background. "Are you in the middle of dinner, Mom?" she asked.

"We're just finishing, honey," Lois answered. "I'm going to take the phone in the den. Hold on just a minute." Lois spoke to Don in the kitchen, then picked up the other phone. Judy heard Don hang up the kitchen phone. "Now we can talk without kitchen noise," she said. "I didn't expect to hear from you until you returned home. How is the honeymoon?"

"It's great, Mom," Judy answered. "The chalet is a dream. Today we went into the White Mountains and drove to the top of Mt. Washington. We've had a wonderful time."

"You don't know how good it is to hear that, Judy," Lois replied.

"Mom, I have a question to ask. Do you have some time to talk?"

"Of course I do. What is it?"

"What was it like for Daddy in the beginning?"

"Judy, is this something that you want to talk about on your honeymoon? It wasn't pleasant."

"I have a reason for asking, Mom."

Lois went cold. She didn't want to continue. She still prayed every day that Judy would be one of the fifty percent of children that was spared. Hoping that this was just an exploratory question, Lois asked, "What is your reason?"

"When Mark and I flew home from visiting you and Dad, I fell in the aisle of the airplane for no apparent reason. Later, as you know, I had a momentary blackout in the Pastor's office. When we arrived in New Hampshire, Mark and I went shopping at the supermarket. He had put some light bulbs in the basket without telling me. I made a scene at the check out, again for no particular reason. Things are happening to me that I can't explain. None of these incidents is serious. It could be clumsiness, fatigue, or something else. I guess that I have been thinking of Daddy so much in recent months that I am alert to anything unusual."

This all sounded so familiar, Lois thought. She and Richard had discounted all of the symptoms in the beginning until they ran out of explanations. They hadn't made the connection between Richard's uncles and Richard. So little was known about Huntington's Disease, and so little had been spoken of Richard's uncles that they had no reason to suspect the cause of his increasingly strange behavior.

"Have you discussed this with Mark or a doctor, Judy?" Lois asked, trying not to alarm her.

"Certainly not!" Judy said with a tone of finality. "How could I ever tell Mark now that I have a fifty-fifty chance of having Huntington's Disease? He would feel betrayed. He wants a family and talks about it all the time. You were right, Mom, when you told me to deal with this before we got married. Now, whether I have the disease or not, I feel trapped."

Lois didn't play the "I told you so" game. She could feel the pain that Judy was already experiencing. "How about a doctor, Judy?" she asked again.

"A doctor would want me to be tested, wouldn't he?"

"It would be the right thing for you to do."

"I don't think that I can face the truth, Mom, but you still haven't answered my question."

"About Richard?" Lois asked.

"Yes, about Richard."

"You want to know about his symptoms. Okay, I'll tell you, but I can't believe that you don't remember. You were there."

"Mom, you know that I retreated into my room and into myself when things got bad. He scared me."

"Richard knew that, too. It hurt him deeply, but he understood. He never lost his intelligence, you know. He was able to reason clearly until the day that he died. That was not always a blessing. Sometimes I wished that he had been less aware of what was going on in his body. Huntington's is merciless and persistent. It takes a long time from the beginning of symptoms until the blessing of death. Some people suffer increasingly for twenty years. It depends on how old you are when the symptoms start. Usually they start around your age, Judy, but occasionally they begin in childhood. Then it is quicker."

"How long did Richard suffer before he died?" Judy asked.

"He only suffered for about five years, but his symptoms began ten years before he died," Lois answered. "Are you sure that you want to know about his symptoms, Judy? Are you sure that you won't obsess every time you experience something that seems like a symptom? Wouldn't it be better for you to be tested and know for certain than to fret over every normal mishap in life?"

"I don't know, Mom," Judy replied. "Perhaps you're right. Could you just tell me whether Richard experienced the things that have happened to me recently?"

There was a pause. Without hearing a word from Lois, Judy knew her answer. In that moment of silence Judy's whole life collapsed. She began to sob, loudly enough for Lois to hear. "I'm so sorry, Judy," her mother said. Judy could hear that her mother, too, was crying.

Through her sobs, Judy thanked her mother and ended the conversation, then sat in the gazebo alone with her thoughts until the sun set. The sun was also going down on her life.

• • •

Mark awoke in the chaise lounge with a cramp in his back, wondering where Judy had gone. She must have taken a walk, he thought. Concerned because it was getting dark, Mark walked to the road in front of the chalet. He could see Judy walking slowly toward him with her head lowered, obviously deep in thought. He called to her and her head snapped up as if she had awakened from a daydream. "Are you all right?" Mark asked.

"Yes," she lied. Taking hold of Mark's arm, she turned him toward the chalet so that he wouldn't see her face. Holding hands they walked quietly together until they got inside.

"Are you brave enough to eat a meal that I prepare?" Mark asked.

"Right now, I'd eat anything," Judy said, trying to sound upbeat. "I'm starved."

George hadn't heard from the blackmailer for a week. He was getting concerned. The Executive Committee was certain that he would be contacted. After learning about Dr. Archer's project they were interested in getting the data disks.

Dr. George Palmer felt that his life was going nowhere. He had lost some credibility at Bio-Gen by mishandling the Archer affair. His marriage had ended in divorce when his wife decided that Bio-Gen was an unbeatable mistress. It had cost him a bundle.

Leaving his car in the garage, he entered the house through a door leading into his workshop. In the kitchen the red light was flashing on his answering machine. Turning on the lamp next to the phone, he saw that there were four messages waiting for him.

Shedding his sport coat and tie, George poured a glass of water, returned to the phone, and pressed the play button. A voice said, "Hello, George. Did you find the disks interesting?" The caller then left a phone number and time when George should return the call. He had spoken to the blackmailer before, but the voice had never registered in his mind. For some reason he was alerted to the voice, but he wasn't sure why. He was to call the following morning at ten o'clock.

• • •

The next day George closed the door to his office and lifted the receiver at the appointed hour, then dialed the number he had been given. The familiar voice answered, "Good morning, George."

"You're pretty sure of yourself, aren't you?" George asked, irritated by the arrogance of the blackmailer.

"I think that I have what you want, right?" the caller asked.

"Perhaps. It depends on your terms. Dr. Archer's story was interesting, but not worth giving the store away," he lied. Bio-Gen would have given the proverbial store away.

"Come on, George. You know that this is big. Let's see, I have eighteen disks all containing gibberish as far as I'm concerned. They could be reformatted and my life would go on as usual. Or, perhaps you can make sense of this gibberish and, just supposing, Bio-Gen could make a lot of money, right?"

"Get to the point," George said.

"All right. I don't like this cat and mouse stuff. It's too risky. I'd like to dispose of the whole lot and be done with it, agreed?"

"Agreed. How much?"

"$10,000 per disk," the voice said firmly.

"You're out of your mind," George responded. The phone went dead. George redialed.

"See, George," the voice said. "You panicked, didn't you?"

"$5,000 per disk," George said. "Take it or leave it."

"You are not in the driver's seat, George. I am. You do not set the price. I do. Let's see, eighteen disks times $5,000 is $90,000. Not enough. I suggest that you round it off to an even $100,000."

"Okay. Try to be a little more creative in the transfer this time. Any kid could have opened that telephone box."

"We've talked long enough, George. I'll be in touch."

George proceeded at once to Aaron Krimer's office and reported the conversation. There was no disagreement over the amount of money. Keith Lawson was instructed to get the money to George before the end of the day.

As George pulled into his driveway he noticed that the red flag on his mailbox was raised. He went to the mailbox, withdrew the day's mail and found an unstamped envelope on the top of the pile. He lowered the flag and juggling mail, a briefcase containing $100,000, and house keys, he entered the house and went immediately into the kitchen. He quickly opened the unstamped envelope. As he suspected it was from the blackmailer. A typed note read, "Make your delivery to the I & M Canal Bicycle Trail. Be alone. Take Willow Springs Road past Archer Avenue. You'll find signs reading 'Parking/Trail Access.' Park in the lot and walk onto the trail. At the entrance turn right and walk a short distance until you see a portable toilet. The toilet is on a skid. There is a small open space in the skid. Place your package there at exactly 2:00 P.M. on Tuesday. Make sure it is in a watertight wrapping. When you have put it in the right place continue walking on the trail for approximately one mile, then return. You will find what you are looking for in the same place."

Tuesday was a sunny day. George placed $100,000 in an empty box, then wrapped the box in plastic. Not being a jogger or a cyclist, he wore Levi's, a short-sleeved shirt, and loafers. With difficulty he located the I&M Canal Bicycle Trail and was immediately intimidated. In addition to cyclists and joggers there were small clusters of tough-looking teens. The young people meant no harm, but to George they were menacing. The fact that he was carrying $100,000 dollars didn't increase his comfort level. George mustered his courage, walked quickly past the first of two groups of teens without exchanging words, then turned right in search of the portable toilet. It was already in sight as he stepped onto the trail. The trail was crowded with cyclists and joggers. George placed the package where he had been told, then continued walking. After fifteen minutes he turned back and returned to the scene of the crime. To his surprise, the package had been replaced by another box. He made the retrieve in a matter of seconds and walked quickly to his car. Once inside, he locked all of the doors and breathed a sigh of relief. Opening the box, he counted eighteen ZIP disks. Speeding out of the parking lot, he headed for Bio-Gen. It was over. He had them all. Or did he? He reported at once to the Chief Executive Officer.

Aaron Krimer III was not a scientist. He depended on doctors Palmer and Phillips to make sense of the data disks. "Take all the time you need, George, to analyze these disks, then I want you to submit a report in non-scientific jargon to the Executive Committee."

George nodded, promising that he and Michele Phillips would prepare a report as soon as possible.

6

Mark kept Judy so busy over the remaining days of their honeymoon that she had little time to think of Huntington's. On one day they visited Franconia Notch State Park and the Flume Gorge. On another they rode horses at the base of Loon Mountain, then took the Summit Skyride to the top. Each evening they drove back to Woodsville. Their last full day came too quickly. There was nothing on the day's agenda, so they changed into their jogging clothes and started up the gravel road toward the ski cabin.

Leaving the chalet, Mark and Judy limbered up in the yard, then headed for the crushed gravel road, turning toward Woodsville. One-quarter mile from the chalet, a well-kept stone road turned off to the right and headed up the foothill. The road meandered through the woods, over two trickling creeks, then ended in a grassy clearing. The clearing was approximately half the size of a football field and served as a parking area. During the skiing season when the lift was operating, skiers would be picked up at a small cabin a short walk from the clearing. Since his family had organized the community association he had no qualms about entering the cabin.

The door opened easily. The wood-burning potbelly stove standing in the center of the room was as cold as the weather outside was hot. On one end of the cabin was a desk used by the lift attendant. In a semi-circle around the potbelly stove stood several mismatched chairs obviously left over from garage sales. One was upholstered and offered a modicum of comfort. Mark fell easily into its welcome embrace. He pulled Judy into his lap. The chair gave a short squeak of resistance, but refused to collapse into pieces.

Content to rest in each other's arms, they remained silent letting their bodies melt into one another. Mark found the smell and feel of Judy's body exciting. He removed her jogging clothes without resistance, and they made intense love on the rough floor of the cabin. Lying in each other's arms afterwards, Mark said, "I can't wait to bring our kids here and teach them to ski." Judy extricated herself from Mark, stood and dressed without a word. "Did I say something wrong?" Mark asked.

"No, Mark, you didn't say anything wrong," Judy said with a tone of assurance and regret. "It's me. I have not been honest with you, Mark, and I can't go on living a lie. I am ashamed and afraid. I don't want to lose you, Mark, but I think that what I am going to say may cause you to be very angry. I wouldn't blame you for leaving."

Mark dressed and went to Judy. He put his hands on her shoulders and looked her squarely in the eyes. "Whatever it is, you can tell me, Judy. There is nothing that could come between us. I love you. Don't you know that?"

"Yes. That's why I'm so ashamed, Mark. I know that you love me, and I love you. I should have trusted our love and had this conversation before we married, but I was so afraid that you wouldn't want to marry me."

Mark pulled Judy into a chair, then arranged another chair directly facing hers. "You must tell me now, Judy, before we leave this cabin," he insisted. There was no threat in his request, only concern. He spoke softly, holding both of Judy's hands.

Looking down into her lap, Judy began almost inaudibly. Mark gently lifted her chin so that she was looking directly at him. She began again. She told him about Richard Hammond, the genetic risks of Huntington's, the seriousness and symptoms of the disease, and the reasons for not bringing children into a Huntington's family. She spoke softly and steadily until she finished, then she looked at Mark waiting for a reaction and not knowing what to expect.

"Do you have this disease?" Mark asked.

"I have never been tested, Mark."

"Is there a test for Huntington's?"

"Yes, and it's reliable."

"Then why haven't you had it?"

Judy explained her reasons, but she knew that there was no good excuse except fear. "Some things have happened recently, Mark, that might be early symptoms—my fall in the airplane, my blackout in Pastor Dressler's office, and my outburst at the supermarket. Mom tells me that Daddy had these same symptoms."

"Then you think that you have the disease?" Mark asked tremulously.

Judy placed her hands on the sides of his face. She could see that he was floundering. Mark's mind went blank. He couldn't grasp at once the implications of what Judy was saying. He stood, removed her hands from his face, and left the cabin. Judy watched as he walked down the path to the grassy clearing and out of sight. She stood at the door of the cabin, her head leaning on the doorframe, alone.

Mark couldn't handle deceit. He felt like an animal that had freed itself from a trap only to walk into another trap. Frozen feelings are the result of feelings mishandled. As a boy his feelings were not allowed. His parents were distracted by their own issues and had little time for the hurts and joys of their son. When his middle school love affair was ended when his girlfriend's family moved to California, he was crushed. His mother found him crying in his bedroom, then told him to grow up and take it like a man. Over time, Mark had learned to keep his feelings to himself until there were no more feelings. Now, as Dr. Lum had predicted, feelings were beginning to stir. Judy awakened in him something wonderful—love, but Mark had just learned his first major lesson about love. It can set you up for a steep fall.

He walked back to the chalet without seeing the beauty of the New Hampshire hills and woods. The sun shining through the pine trees, the sounds of birds, the trickling creeks were just peripheral images in his watery eyes as he walked slowly, head down, on automatic pilot. When he arrived at the chalet he went into the backyard, picked up pieces of firewood lying outside the screened-in porch and threw them as far as he could until he was exhausted. His pent-up rage dissipated, he entered the chalet. He wasn't able to process what Judy had said, but he had dealt with the anger. Processing would come later.

Judy found him packing when she returned to the chalet. She had taken a detour by way of the pond and sat in the gazebo watching the children on the sandy beach. There were no more tears. She had drained the well dry. All she felt was sadness and uncertainty. What could she say now? What was left to say? It was now up to Mark, and she didn't know what to expect.

The silence was unbearable for both of them. They drove 1,100 miles with one overnight stop. Judy's attempts to get Mark to talk were met with polite refusals. It wasn't until they were in Illinois that Mark announced, "Judy, I'm going to stay at my apartment for a few days until I sort this out. I hope you understand. Don't draw any long-term conclusions from this. I love you, and I'm sure that we can work this out, but I need a little more time."

There were enough assurances in Mark's announcement to give Judy hope. "I do understand, Mark. I want to work this out, too, but not until you are ready. Please don't take too long," she appealed.

Mark swapped cars at the rental agency and repacked the luggage into his police vehicle, then he and Judy proceeded to their townhouse. After unloading Judy's luggage, Mark hugged Judy for a long time, then drove to the Tetlow's.

Mark hadn't been to the police station since his promotion. When he entered the building on the morning after his return from New Hampshire he was shocked to see a banner above the reception desk reading, "Welcome Lieutenant Garrison!" Sue greeted him first, hugging him, then Jeff Myers extended his hand. Corky was on assignment.

In the early afternoon he called Sue to the interrogation room. Handing her a slip of paper with the telephone numbers of Dr. Lum and Dr. Spencer, he said, "Sue, I need for you to make two appointments for me."

Dr. Lum was sitting in a lawn chair on the front porch of his house. He waved as Mark stepped out of his police car, motioning for Mark to join him on the porch. "Hi," Mark said as he climbed the porch steps. "I'm surprised to get an appointment so soon. Our clerk just called this morning."

"I'm off this week, Mark," Lum said. "My office is being redecorated. I want to brighten it up some."

"Thanks for seeing me."

"How are things going?"

"Judy and I were married a week and half ago and just returned from our honeymoon."

"Congratulations."

"The last time we met you said that if Judy were the right girl she would help me expand my range of feelings. You were right. She is the right girl, and I have discovered new feelings. The problem is that they aren't all good, and I'm not sure how to deal with some of them. I'm confused, to say the least."

"Start at the beginning, Mark," Lum suggested.

"I've known that I loved Judy from the day I met her, the day I had to tell her about her husband's death. As strange as it seems, I think she loved me from that moment, too, her grief notwithstanding. Our honeymoon was great. Being with her is the best thing that's ever happened to me."

"Then why are you here?"

Mark looked away from Dr. Lum. It was difficult for him to put the events of the past several days into words. Perhaps that's why he felt he needed to see Dr. Lum. Right now, Lum was the only person in his life that he could trust absolutely. "Judy told me on the last day of our stay in New Hampshire that her biological father died of Huntington's Disease, and that she suspects that she may be experiencing symptoms of the same disease."

This time Lum looked away. He had counseled Huntington's patients and their families on several occasions, and he was familiar with the disease. "She had never mentioned this before? Did you not discuss her family of origin?"

"Only her present family. I didn't know that her stepfather wasn't her biological father until we applied for our marriage license. Even then she told me that her biological father had died of an illness without going into detail. I didn't think to ask any questions."

"Why do you think that she withheld this information, Mark?"

"I'm not sure."

"Think about it," Lum pushed. "What would have happened if she had told you that she might have inherited a dreadful terminal disease?"

"That I wouldn't have married her?"

"Is that true?"

"I don't know," Mark admitted.

"This is the decision you have to face now, Mark."

"I guess I've known that, Dr. Lum."

"Good, Mark. When you make the decision you will know how to proceed in your relationship with Judy," Dr. Lum said, standing. Mark wasn't going to get help with the decision. That was clear. He stood and shook hands with Dr. Lum. "Call me if you need to, Mark," Lum said as Mark headed towards his car.

Mark knew what he had to do. He had never heard of Huntington's Disease until Judy spoke of it. Mark called from his mobile phone to see whether Sue had gotten an appointment with Dr. Spencer. "Tomorrow morning at 9:00 A.M. at Marge's," Sue said. "Does that work for you?"

"Tell Captain Myers that I'll be clocking in late tomorrow, Sue, and that he can reach me at my mobile phone. And put the name and phone number of the crew leader who cleaned up on the evening that the Archer evidence disappeared from my desk in my office, please."

"Why?" Sue asked. Mark was surprised at her question. She rarely questioned Mark's requests.

"Because I'm still trying to locate the missing disks, Sue," Mark said.

"I thought the Archer case was closed," Sue persisted.

"It is officially, but I'm still interested. Why are you asking?" Mark asked. Ignoring his question, she promised to leave the name and number of the cleanup crew chief.

Mark arrived at the station early the following morning intending to pick up the information about the cleanup crew chief and then head to Marge's to meet Dr. Spencer. As promised, the name and number were on a yellow stick-on note next to his phone. On his way to Marge's he dialed the number from his mobile phone. A very angry lady answered. "Do you know what time it is?" she asked.

"8:30 in the morning."

"Who is this?" she said, still bristling.

"This is Lieutenant Mark Garrison of the Riverside Police Department. May I speak to Mister Rawlings, please?"

"There ain't no Rawlings here," she said. The phone went dead. Mark was puzzled. The name on the yellow note was Dale Rawlings. Mark dialed again, thinking that he had called the wrong number. When the same angry voice answered he hung up.

Dr. Spencer was already in a booth at Marge's when Mark arrived. Ed Braun was at the counter. Mark took a detour on the way to Dr. Spencer's booth and greeted Ed.

"Caught a few on my new rod and reel," Ed said. "Thanks."

"Don't mention it," Mark replied. "Do you remember the cleanup crew chief that you talked to about the disks?"

"Yes, Dale, I think he called himself."

"Do you have his phone number or address?" Mark asked.

"Not here," he replied, "but I can get it for you."

"Leave the information with Sue, will you, Ed?" Mark asked. "She gave me a wrong number for Dale." He patted Ed on the back and headed for Spencer's booth.

"Sure thing," Ed replied.

"Good morning, Dr. Spencer," Mark said as he slid into the booth next to the large, silver-haired man.

"Good morning, Lieutenant," Spencer said with a smile. "Congratulations. I didn't know that Riverside was big enough for two lieutenants."

"I was surprised, too," said Mark. "I thought I'd have to wait until Corky died. Looks like the department is going to expand some."

"Is that because Riverside is growing or because there is more crime?" Dr. Spencer asked.

"The former," Mark replied. "How is everything with you?"

"Boring," Spencer said. "I'm running out of things to do in my retirement."

"Maybe I can help," Mark offered. "I need some information—medical information."

"What's wrong, Mark?" Spencer asked. Mark told the doctor about Judy's situation.

"I'm not as up on Huntington's as I could be," Spencer confessed. "I'll have to do some reading, then get back to you. As far as I can remember we've only had one family in Riverside with Huntington's. It wasn't long after I started my practice. Very little was known about the disease then. I treated the symptoms for years until the lady died. She was the last member of the family to have the disease and there hasn't been another case here."

"Is it fatal?" Mark asked.

"Always," Spencer answered. "No cure, as far as I know, but I'll get caught up on the research before we meet again."

"How long will it take?"

"Is tomorrow soon enough?" Spencer answered. "I don't have a lot on my calendar these days. I can spend the afternoon at my computer and call a few colleagues. How about meeting here for breakfast?"

"If you don't mind I'd rather not meet here. Would you be willing to come to my apartment at Tetlow's? We can have breakfast there."

"I'll see you at ten, Mark. Just coffee. I'd hate to break Marge's heart."

"Thanks, Doctor."

On the chance that he could catch Ed at the railroad station, Mark headed in that direction. He got lucky. Ed was sweeping behind the ticket counter. As Mark entered the station, Ed said, "I left the number you wanted with Sue."

"Great. Thanks. That's why I dropped by. Did you also give her an address?"

"Didn't have one. I talked to Dale over the phone."

"Do you have his number here, Ed?" Mark asked. Ed pulled a note from his pocket and handed it to Mark. "Thanks, Ed. I'll call Dale and get his address."

Mark returned to his car and compared Ed's number with the number on the yellow stick-on note from Sue. It was different by one digit. He called the number that Ed had given him, and got Dale Rawlings. After identifying himself, he got directions to Dale's house.

Rawlings came to the door of his small Cape Cod style house. He was in a bathrobe and slippers. "Garrison?" he asked.

"Yes," Mark said, and showed him his identification.

"Come in," Rawlings said, opening the door into a neat living room.

"I hope I didn't wake you."

"You did. I work nights," Rawlings replied in a friendly tone.

"Sorry," Mark apologized.

"What's up?"

"I'll make this short," Mark began. "I know several people have asked you about a carton that was moved to the trash bin after the death of Bob Archer. Recently you told Ed Braun that there was a note attached to the carton. Is that correct?"

"Yep," Rawlings answered.

Mark took the yellow stick-on note on which Sue had written Rawlings information. "Was it a note paper like this?"

"Yep," Rawlings answered, taking Mark's note.

"What was written on it?"

"Trash," Rawlings said.

"That's it?" Mark asked. "Just 'trash'?"

"That's it," Rawlings replied. "So we took it out with the trash."

"Did you or anyone on the crew open the box?" Mark asked.

"We don't inspect trash," Rawlings said. "We just get rid of it."

"How much did the carton weigh?"

"I really don't remember. It wasn't heavy, if that's what you mean."

"Can you remember anything else?"

"Not really."

"I really appreciate your willingness to meet with me, and I'm sorry that I woke you up," Mark said.

"Hope it helps," Rawlings said, walking with Mark to the door.

"Me, too."

Mark stopped at Dunkin' Donuts on his way to the police station. After getting his usual assortment for the break room, he sat in the parking lot without starting his engine. His head was swimming. Judy, Huntington's, and missing disks were swirling about in his mind. He had to focus. Sort things out, he told himself. He would call Judy and arrange to meet her for lunch. Dr. Spencer would have information about Huntington's tomorrow. Now, at this moment, he would concentrate on the missing disks.

The last time Mark had seen the disks they were in the evidence room.

Sue moved them to his desk because they weren't marked properly when she took her monthly inventory of evidence. The cleanup crew moved them to the trash bin during their nighttime cleanup. The trash bin was empty on the following day when they were needed. Sue had said that the cleanup crew took them by mistake, but the cleanup crew chief said that there was a yellow stick-on note reading "trash" on the box—like the note that Sue had left for Mark. Who but Sue could have placed a note on the box? And how could she forget doing it? In fact, Sue had forgotten several things lately, and had given Mark the wrong phone number for the cleanup crew chief. Mark had also noticed changes in Sue's life, including a new wardrobe and a new car.

As Mark entered the police station, he stopped by Sue's desk and invited her into his office area in the interrogation room. "I'd like to speak with you for a minute, Sue," Mark said as she stepped into the room.

"Sure, Mark," Sue said. He closed the door behind her.

"Sue, did Ed Braun call this morning?" Mark asked, knowing the answer.

"Not that I'm aware of," Sue replied.

"Has anyone else been taking calls on the phone today, Sue?"

"I don't think so," Sue responded after a pause.

"You'd better have a seat, Sue," Mark said, pulling a straight-back chair away from the interrogation table. "Tell me again what happened to the Archer disks."

"What's going on, Mark?" Sue asked. "We've been through this and the issue has been put to rest."

"Not entirely, Sue. Those disks are still very important to a lot of people. The department has closed the Archer investigation, but I'm trying to wrap up this one loose end. I need for you to go over it with me one more time."

"Mark, I know that you have my story on record. I transcribed all of your tapes, remember? Why not just read my report?"

"Is there some reason that you don't want to answer my question, Sue?"

"I'm getting bad vibes, that's all."

"Start at the beginning, Sue," Mark said, losing patience.

Sue gazed at Mark with a look that he had never seen before. After a decade and a half of police work, he knew the defensive postures of the accused. "I don't think that I want to do this, Mark," she said.

"I'll tell you then, Sue, that I'm not asking out of idle curiosity. I have reason to think that you have not told me the truth about the disappearance of the disks." He didn't mention the missing phone messages, altered phone number for Dale Rawlings, or the "trash" note.

"That's it, Mark. I'm not saying anything further. I don't like what you're doing. I thought that we were friends, and you come on like I did something wrong." She stood up and started to leave the room. Mark stepped between her and the door, convinced that she was hiding something.

"This is not it, Sue. I want you to go home and think about what has happened here. When you come in tomorrow be ready to answer my question."

"Am I being fired?" she asked.

"Take a personal day, Sue," Mark answered. He stepped aside and allowed her to leave the interrogation room.

Mark went straight to Jeff Myers' office. He was on the phone but beckoned Mark to enter and pointed to a chair alongside his desk. Placing the phone on the cradle, he said, "Morning, Mark. What's up?"

"I think we have a problem, Jeff," Mark started. "It might be best if Corky were here, too."

"Get Corky and a donut and coffee for me, Mark," Jeff said. In a moment the three were assembled around the Captain's desk. "Your show, Mark," Jeff said.

Beginning at the night that the disks disappeared, Mark shared his suspicions about Sue's involvement in the matter, including her recent omissions and errors. Then, looking at Jeff, he asked, "Have you given Sue a raise recently?"

"No," Jeff answered. "Why do you ask?"

"She's living above her income," Mark replied. "Have you looked at her clothes, her appearance, her new Beemer?"

"What has this to do with the missing disks?" Corky asked.

"I'm not sure," Mark admitted, "but I believe that it's more than coincidence that she is somehow connected with the missing disks and is now living above her means."

"Have you talked with her, Mark?" Jeff asked.

"Yes, just a while ago. She became defensive. She wouldn't discuss the issue of the disks. I sent her home on personal leave."

"I'll call the town attorney," Jeff offered. "Mark, you contact Sue and put her on indefinite administrative leave until we decide what to do next." Mark and Corky stood to leave the office. "I hope you're right about this, Mark," Jeff said. "Sue has been a solid citizen here and has a long family history of police work."

"I hope I'm wrong, Jeff," Mark countered, then left.

Sue wasn't home when Mark called. He left a message on her answering machine, then called Judy at the townhouse. It was his first contact since returning from New Hampshire. She answered on the first ring. Mark hadn't rehearsed what he would say, and now he wished he had. "Hello," she said.

"Hi," he replied, then went blank.

Judy came to Mark's rescue. "I'm glad you called."

"Can we have lunch together today?" he asked.

"Yes, when can you come over?" she replied.

"Let's meet at Marge's," Mark said.

"I'd rather meet at the park. It's a beautiful day. I'll make a picnic," Judy offered.

"Noon?"

"Noon."

Judy was waiting when Mark arrived. Lunch was set up on a picnic table. "I miss you," he said.

"I miss you, too. How long, Mark?" she asked.

"Not long," he answered. "How are you doing?"

"Keeping busy," she answered. "School starts in a week. I'm getting my room set up and buying supplies. How about you?"

"I've seen Dr. Lum, and I'm going to see Dr. Spencer to learn more about Huntington's."

"I don't know as much as I should about Huntington's. Perhaps you could share what you learn," Judy asked.

"Have you had any more episodes?"

"No. I know that I should have told you about Huntington's, Mark, and I'm sorry," Judy said.

"Let's have lunch," Mark said, leaving the issue hanging.

Judy said, "It doesn't seem right, us being newlyweds and living apart."

"I've started packing some things, Judy. As soon as Dr. Spencer and I have met, I'll be moving to the townhouse, but there are issues for us to work out. I will not give up on having a family, and there can be no more secrets."

Judy took Mark's face in her hands and looked straight into his eyes. "Not telling you about Huntington's is the biggest mistake I've ever made, Mark. Nothing like that will happen again. If I have Huntington's I will not pass those genes along, but that doesn't rule out adoption."

"What hurts most is the deception, the lack of trust."

"Forgive me, Mark."

"I do forgive you, Judy." They held each other for a long time before going their separate ways.

The next day Mark tidied his apartment for Dr. Spencer's visit, had a light breakfast of toast and V8, and made a pot of coffee. Spencer arrived on time. "I did some research, Mark," Spencer said as Mark poured a mug of coffee, then pointed to the sugar and milk on the table. Spencer shook his head and sipped from the mug. "I believe I can answer your questions about Huntington's, but only in broad strokes. I haven't read the important journal reports."

"How bad is it?" Mark asked.

"As bad as it gets." Then Dr. Spencer told Mark in laymen's terms what lay ahead for Judy.

"Judy thinks that there is a test that can diagnose Huntington's. Is that true?" Mark asked.

"Yes," Spencer answered. "But being tested is a very personal thing. Has Judy expressed an interest in being tested?"

"She refuses," Mark answered.

"I'm not surprised, Mark," Spencer said. "For some people, the uncertainty of whether they carry the faulty gene is stressful and distracting. For others the knowledge that they will develop the condition is burdensome. Can I make a suggestion?"

"Of course," Mark replied.

"Ask Judy whether she would be willing to talk to me. Her symptoms can be the result of many conditions. They don't necessarily mean she has Huntington's Disease. I should add that with her family history, I wouldn't get your hopes up."

"What does the testing involve?" Mark asked.

"I would perform a physical exam and get Judy's medical and family history. I'd also need for her to tell me about any recent emotional or intellectual changes she has had. It is doubtful that she has told you every-thing, or that you have seen all of her symptoms. A CT scan or an MRI may show changes to her brain's structure. I would also request a blood test to determine whether she carries the defective gene."

"How much care would Judy require, Dr. Spencer?"

"Most Huntington patients need help with personal care and feeding. There is one other thing that caregivers need to know, Mark."

"And that is?"

"Huntington's patients commit suicide at a rate seven times greater than the regular population," Spencer warned. "A caregiver has to be on the alert for this, especially in the case of those patients who have experienced the disease in their family and seen its devastation." He reached across the table and put his hand on Mark's.

"If Judy is willing, would you take care of her?" Mark asked.

"Yes, of course, Mark, but I'm an old man and Judy's symptoms, if they are Huntington's, are just beginning. They could go on for several decades. I won't be around that long. I'll do what I can."

"Thanks, Dr. Spencer," Mark said. Spencer gathered his notes and headed for the door. Mark remained seated at the table, looking down.

"Mark, are you a praying man?" Spencer asked.

"Sometimes."

"Then get busy."

Mark had known before Dr. Spencer arrived what he would do. He loved Judy. He would return to her and keep his vows "in sickness and in health." Spencer's visit had been helpful. Now Mark understood the burden Judy was carrying, and he could forgive her deceit. He left the kitchen and went to a storage cabinet on the rear porch of his apartment. Removing all of the suitcases from the cabinet, he carried them into his bedroom, then began packing for the move to the townhouse.

7

The daughter of a retired city policeman, Susan McGrath was employed by the Riverside Police Department two months after graduating from high school. She had been the department clerk ever since. Her dreams of becoming an officer in the RPD were ended when Dr. Spencer detected a heart murmur during her physical examination. Unable to follow in her father's footsteps, she settled on the desk job. In addition to her love for police work she had her father's Irish spirit. She was feisty, fun, and full of energy. Mark and Susan had become close friends during their years on the force. She always gave the impression of being pleased with her work.

At Captain Myers' instructions, Lieutenant Corcoran placed Sue on administrative leave with pay until Mark's suspicions could be cleared up. Sue spent the first two days of her leave packing her things. On the third day she signed a lease for a small house in an older section of Riverside. Determined to use this time to her advantage she began moving her things into the house as soon as the lease was signed.

Although Sue had been the department clerk for fourteen years, she had never received more than a cost-of-living pay increase. Knowing the risk of complaining, she bore her resentment quietly. Now, at last, she could afford a decent car, decent clothes, and a place of her own. There is no way they would ever discover what she had done with the disks, she thought, and the copies she made would keep that idiot George from talking, if it became necessary to use them. Now she had to keep her cool. She knew she had made a mistake spending the money so soon. She had also been stupid to try to interfere with Ed Braun's messages, but none of these things proved anything. The dumbest thing of all, Sue thought, was not insisting on more money from George. It was clear from Mark's cassette tapes that Archer's work was important, but it wasn't until she read the narrative disks that she knew how valuable they were. Sue assumed that George would destroy the disks as soon as he got his hands on them in order to protect Bio-Gen. Now, she wasn't so sure. It was too easy. He was too willing to pay. She should have demanded more. It wasn't too late. She had her own backups.

Getting settled into a house was not quite as easy as moving into an apartment. Sue knew nothing about the mechanical equipment in the house she had rented. She had always left that to her landlord. Under her new lease she was responsible for maintenance. The older frame house was situated on a small lot adjacent to a wooded park in the rear. It needed redecorating, but that would wait until things settled down at the police station. She was certain that she would be back to work in a day or so. As soon as the movers unloaded the last pieces of furniture Sue headed for Home Depot with a list of things to buy, including a lawn mower, a gas can, and a string trimmer.

Lieutenants Corcoran and Garrison arrived at Captain Myers' office at the same time. Jeff motioned to them to be seated. "I've spoken to the town attorney about Sue. She says that we do not have sufficient cause to take any action. Technically, this is not a case of evidence tampering because the evidence was not properly identified, and because the case had been officially closed when Dr. Spencer declared Archer's death a suicide."

"You mean that someone can steal disks from the police department and get away with it?" Corky asked. "And where is she getting the money to support her new lifestyle?"

"We have no solid evidence that Sue stole the disks, Corky," Jeff said. "We can't prove that she put the trash note on the box. She could claim that anyone could have done that. Besides, unless we can establish their value we have nothing more than the petty theft of a box of disks, probably not worth $100. As to her lifestyle, unless we have good cause we can't search her financial records."

"Something isn't right about this," Mark said.

"I can't act on your suspicion, Mark," Jeff said. "The town attorney wants facts. She suggests that we call Sue back to work and keep our eyes on her."

"It won't be the same when she returns, Jeff. You know that," Mark said.

"We have no choice, Mark. The attorney says that we have no grounds to fire Sue, and she can make things hot if we try," Jeff replied. "Sue probably took the disks. What she did with them is anyone's guess, but we can not accuse her with what we have. Is that clear to everyone?" Jeff asked.

Corky and Mark nodded. "Who's going to call her?" Corky asked, hoping to delegate upwards.

"She reports to you," Jeff said, looking at Lieutenant Corcoran.

"I'll call her apartment now," Corky said, turning to leave. He returned to his desk and dialed Sue's number. To his surprise there was no answer either from Sue or her answering machine.

Doctors Palmer and Phillips were amazed that Dr. Archer had been able to develop a remedy for the defect in Gene 15105. They knew his reputation in the field of genetic research, but what they discovered on his data disks astounded them. In a sense, they were growing more sympathetic to Dr. Archer's clandestine human trials. It would have taken years to work through animal testing, then get approval for human testing. Archer's work couldn't wait. Finding a corrective for a gene mutation that effected the aggregate health of every human being was like finding a pot of gold at the end of every geneticist's rainbow. As a bonus, the corrective was not exotic and could be produced in quantity at a reasonable cost.

Approaching the end of their review of Archer's data disks, their excitement grew. "This is more than I expected," Michele said.

"The Executive Committee wanted to assess the liabilities attached to Archer's work, but they have no idea of the potential that his work has for Bio-Gen's future," George replied. "We need to get this evaluation to them as soon as possible."

George called Aaron Krimer and requested a meeting with the Executive Committee. "Dr. Phillips and I have completed our review of the data disks. We have not replicated Dr. Archer's work in the laboratory. That will take some time, but I think that the Executive Committee should hear what we've learned up to this point."

"George, I'm just pleased that the disks are in house. Unless you have learned something that we can exploit for our own benefit, you have permission to destroy the disks and get back to your assignments. You have made certain that there are no copies anywhere, right?"

"I was assured that there were no copies," George said.

"We have done this dance before, George," the CEO warned. "Make certain that there are no surprises this time. Do you understand?"

George had no way of knowing whether the blackmailer had made copies. He had accepted the assurance that he had the only remaining set of disks. He wanted to believe that the last evidence of Archer's work was now in house, and that Bio-Gen was no longer at risk, but could he be sure?

Doctors Palmer and Phillips presented their findings to the Executive Committee the next morning. The Committee made three decisions. First, Archer's work would be replicated in the laboratory. Second, if the results were satisfactory, a decision would be made whether to begin a formal research project. Third, the name "Archer" would be dropped from all references to the work. George and Michele were dismissed to begin the laboratory confirmation. The Executive Committee remained in session to discuss Bio-Gen's response if the blackmailer made new demands.

While Sue was on administrative leave, Mark had also been packing. On the day after Dr. Spencer described Huntington's, Mark called Judy. She agreed to come to his apartment for dinner. His living room was crammed with suitcases and cardboard boxes. Tetlow's agreed to buy Mark's furniture with the exception of his recliner. The only things that Mark had not packed were his linens and kitchen utensils.

While he waited for Judy to arrive for dinner he was rummaging through two boxes of memorabilia that had been stored in a cabinet in Tetlow's basement. He let his mind drift back to earlier times as he unpacked high school yearbooks, Army insignia, and pictures of his police academy graduating class. One small book caught his attention. He remembered his mother giving him the book when he was a child, but he couldn't remember whether he had ever read it. The binding was stiff as he opened it, but the pages were still in good shape. On the front flyleaf was one printed sentence, "To my son Mark whom I love with all my heart, Mother." Mark stared at the sentence for a long time before turning to the next page. The book was a fictional story about a young family, entitled, "And The Greatest of These." The story was told in the first person by a mother experiencing the joys and challenges of raising her family during the years of the Great Depression. It was a story of survival and sacrifice as a tightly bound family strove together to make ends meet without losing their faith or integrity.

Mark began to read the book and wondered why he had never read it before. Was it because he had such anger toward his mother because of her drinking and carousing? Was it possible that his self-righteous judgment had kept him from ever really knowing his mother? He began to wonder whether the book was autobiographical. Was she writing about his family, but in a different time and place? He vowed to read the book to the end and to revisit his thoughts about his mother. On the verge of being overwhelmed by new feelings, he set the book aside, closed the boxes of memorabilia, and began to prepare dinner.

Judy was right on time, as usual. Both wanted this to be a time for renewal. After dinner, Mark took Judy by the hand and led her out of the kitchen into the cluttered living room. He didn't have a collection of romantic CD's or tapes, so he scanned the AM stations until he got danceable music. Stepping out of her shoes Judy assumed a dance position, but Mark placed her arms around his waist. They swayed to the music until it stopped, then stood in each other's arms until the next song began. They continued their radio dancing for several more songs until Judy led Mark into his bedroom.

The next morning, while they were on their way to Judy's townhouse with the first load of boxes from Mark's apartment, Mark heard the report on the scanner in his police vehicle. Through the static Mark could hear the

Riverside Fire Department dispatchers directing fire vehicles to the older part of town. Then Mark's police radio snapped to attention. The RPD dispatcher was trying to locate him. He responded and was directed to assist the RFD at a house fire. Mark flashed his lights and honked his horn to get Judy's attention. She pulled to the curb, and Mark walked to her Escort. "I have to respond to an emergency in Riverside," he said. "Since we're only a few blocks from the townhouse, I'll unload my boxes in the foyer and head back to town. I'll call you when I find out what's going on."

"Go ahead, Mark," Judy replied. "I'll unpack what we've got until I hear from you."

Mark activated the emergency lights in his police vehicle and sped toward the townhouse. He unloaded his boxes in a few minutes, then returned to Riverside.

When he arrived at the scene of the fire he was still wearing Levi's and a tee shirt. He attached his badge to a lanyard and slipped it over his head, then reported to the Commander on the scene. Officers from the RPD were already diverting traffic at each end of the street. Riverside had three fire stations and equipment from all of them were on the scene, but they hadn't been able to save much of the burning house. "We're just containing the fire right now, Mark," the Fire Commander said, "trying to keep it from spreading to the woods in the back and to the house on the west side."

"It looks like the house is totaled," Mark said.

"It was pretty advanced when we arrived," the Commander said. "The call came from a lady in the house next door who could see flames coming through the garage roof. It went up in a hurry."

"Anyone inside?" Mark asked.

"We don't know yet. We couldn't go in, Mark," the Commander replied. "The neighbor said that someone had just rented the place. She didn't know anything about the new tenant but saw a local mover there yesterday. Nobody has shown up since we arrived. We asked your captain to locate the owner. We'll go in as soon as we can, but there isn't going to be much left."

"How can I help?" Mark asked.

"Just keep the traffic under control. That's it for now," the Commander replied.

Mark checked with the officers at each end of the block, then called Captain Myers. "Jeff, this is Mark. I just talked to the Fire Commander. He tells me that you are trying to locate the owner of the house. Any luck?"

"No, Mark. I've spoken to the owners of record, but they lease the house through a realtor. I'm trying now to get past an answering machine at the agency to get the name of the renter. If you aren't needed there, why don't you drive to the agency and see if you can get something. It's Patrick Real Estate on Center Street."

"The RFD is about done here, Jeff, and the equipment should be gone in several hours. All we're doing is diverting traffic. I'll see if I can get anything from Patrick Real Estate."

The real estate agency was in a small storefront office next to the River-side National Bank on Center Street. The windows were cluttered with pictures of properties being offered for sale, but Mark could see that there were no lights on in the office. There were no signs showing hours of operation or whether the office was open or closed. Mark tapped on the door, not expecting a response. He got none. Returning to his car, he called Jeff on his mobile phone. "I struck out at the real estate office," he said.

"You might as well go back to moving your stuff," Jeff said. "I'll have Sue's replacement keep trying until we come up with something. There is one other thing that you can do, Mark, if you will. Corky has not been able to reach Sue to get her back to work. She is not answering her phone and her machine is not picking up. Stop by her apartment, will you?"

"Sure, Jeff," Mark said. He didn't relish the idea of seeing Sue. His gut told him that she had taken the disks and gotten herself into mischief with them. Besides, she reported to Corky. He had been given the assignment. Nevertheless, Mark headed for her apartment.

Sue lived on the second floor of a brick apartment building. There were four apartments, two on the ground level and two above. Tenants shared a common entrance. Each keyed mailbox on the foyer wall included a buzzer and two-way speaker to that apartment. Tenants' names were typed or written on small pieces of paper and slipped into slots on the mailboxes. Sue's apartment was 2A, but there was no name in the slot. Mark pushed the speaker button but got no response. He climbed the stairs to the apartment and knocked on the door. No response. He knocked louder. Still no response. After a few minutes a lady opened the door of 2B and stepped into the hallway. "If you're looking for Sue she has moved," the lady offered.

Mark was surprised. He didn't remember Sue saying anything about moving. "Do you know where she's gone?"

"She didn't even say goodbye. Just packed up and left," the lady said.

"When did she move?" Mark asked.

"Yesterday," the lady answered.

"Did she use movers?" Mark asked.

"She sure did," the lady answered. "They made a racket and messed up the carpeting." She pointed to the carpeting in the hallway. "I had to call the landlord."

"Do you remember the name of the moving company?" Mark asked.

"Sure do. U-Pack," she said.

Mark thanked the lady and called Jeff Myers from his car. "Jeff, check U-Pack Movers. They moved Sue out of her apartment yesterday. They may be able to tell you where she's living. Did she say anything to you about moving?"

"No," Jeff said. "I'll check with U-Pack. If there is anything else, I'll call you. Otherwise, get back to moving your own things, and thanks."

Mark called Judy on his mobile phone, then drove to the townhouse. He rang the bell. When Judy answered the door he took her by the hand and led her outside onto the porch. He swept her off of her feet and carried her over the threshold. "How many times are you going to do this?" Judy asked, laughing.

"This is the first time I've carried you over the threshold of *our* house," he said, "and this time I'm going to stay." It was a commitment, and Judy understood the meaning.

"You know what this could mean, Mark," she said.

"Yes," he said. "It means that you are stuck with me—for better or for worse." They made three more trips with both cars, ordered a pizza, then slept like logs.

Judy was lying with her head on Mark's chest when his mobile phone rang. Mark reached across Judy and took the phone from the nightstand. "Yes?" he said.

"Mark, you'd better get down here," said Corky.

"Corky? What's up? Where are you?" Mark asked, his head in a daze.

"At the house that burned yesterday, Mark. It was Sue's," Corky answered.

Mark sat upright. "What do you mean Sue's?" he asked.

"Sue moved in the day before yesterday. She was renting it," Corky said.

"Was she in the house?" Mark asked.

"I don't know, Mark."

"I'm on my way," Mark said.

"What did he say?" Judy asked.

"Sue McGrath had just moved into the house that burned yesterday," Mark said.

"What? Was Sue in the house when it burned?" Judy asked.

"No one knows. The Arson Investigator and Corky are there now. I'm going to meet with them," Mark said as he started to rise. Judy pulled him back down to the bed and kissed his shoulder.

8

Aaron Krimer III summoned George to the Bio-Gen conference room. When George entered the room, Krimer, Rory Sanders, and Keith Lawson were already seated. All rose and greeted George then sat down. "We're waiting for the Research Director, George," Sanders said. "How is your family?"

George had not been treated with this kind of courtesy since the Archer affair. At times he wondered whether he was on thin ice at Bio-Gen. "We want to speak with you, George, before the Research Director arrives," Krimer said. "We know that we have put you in some very awkward situations regarding the Archer disks. What we have done to procure the disks would seem inappropriate to outsiders, George, and perhaps to you. We, too, are conflicted about this. We were not all in agreement about the way that we went about getting the disks, but there is one thing on which we must all agree. The manner in which Dr. Archer pursued his project could have ruined this business. On the other hand, the work that he did is very important. The disks describe the inappropriate way that he did his work, but they also give us a remarkable remedy for what appears to be a milieu of conditions affecting a large number of people, if not everyone. Having possession of these disks not only protects our business, but gives us an opportunity to move Dr. Archer's project forward in the proper way. We will never be able to give Dr. Archer the credit he is due for his work because of the way he conducted his research, but all of us in this room know where the credit for this important work belongs. Now we have several questions for you, George."

George was uncomfortable. He shifted in his chair but looked steadily at Krimer. It was, however, the COO who spoke next. "First, George, we want to be assured that there are no copies of these disks unaccounted for. Can you give us that assurance?"

"Yes," George answered. "I can assure you that there are no copies."

"Good," Sanders continued. "We have delayed directing the Research Department to begin work on Dr. Archer's project until we had your assurance. The second question is whether we can count on you to keep the manner in which Dr. Archer developed his project a matter for this Executive Committee and no one else."

"You have my word on this," George said. He wondered if he was going to be asked to mix his blood with theirs. "How will this be kept from the Research Department?"

Krimer answered. "They will not have access to Dr. Archer's narrative disks. They will only receive the data disks that contain the scientific work done by Dr. Archer. His experimentation on the two human subjects are not discussed in the data disks." Turning to the others, Krimer suggested that it was time to call the Research Director into the meeting. "Is there anything else that you would like to discuss, George?"

"No," he answered.

"You may leave, George, and we will continue our meeting with the Research Director," the CEO said, standing. The others also stood and extended their best wishes to George as he left the conference room.

Fire Department tape circled the remains of the house. Ten feet of brick fireplace stood guard over the destroyed building. A smell of smoke hung in the air. Neighbors were walking past, some stopping to look. Trees hanging over the house were singed. One tanker was still in the front yard. Two firemen were spraying embers as Mark parked in front of the house. Corky and the Fire Inspector walked over to Mark's car. "Any sign of Sue?" Mark asked as he stepped from the vehicle.

"We have the remains of one person in the garage," the Inspector said, "but we can't make an identification. We're waiting for Dr. Spencer." As Coroner, it would be up to Spencer to identify the body. Mark couldn't remember a fire death in Riverside. He didn't know how much experience Dr. Spencer had identifying burned bodies.

"Is it an adult?" Mark asked.

"The body appears to be fully grown," the inspector said.

"The RFD has called for a full arson investigation, Mark," Corky added.

"An arson investigation? Why?" Mark asked.

"Standard procedure when there is a death and no obvious cause for the fire," the inspector offered.

"Mark, that car looks like what's left of Sue's Beemer," Corky said, pointing to the burned out shell of a vehicle in what had been the garage. "I'm not going to be surprised at Spencer's findings."

"We should notify someone in her family, just in case," Mark said.

"I'll call Jeff. He can call her father. I don't remember Sue talking about any other family members," Corky responded. "What if it isn't Sue in there? Are we jumping the gun?"

"The fire will be in the paper, Corky," Mark said. "Certainly Sue told him about her move. I'd rather he heard it from us. Are you going to wait for Dr. Spencer?"

"Yes, I'll wait," Corky answered. Mark headed for the station.

It wasn't until after noon that Corky returned to the station. He asked Mark to join him in Captain Myers' office. When the two lieutenants were seated in front of Myers' desk, Jeff asked, "What is the situation regarding Sue, Corky?"

"Dr. Spencer removed the remains," Corky began. "He took them to the clinic for examination. He said that he should have no difficulty identifying the person if dental records can be located. It would be helpful if we could find out from Sue's father which dentist she visited."

Jeff called Sue's replacement into the office and asked for Sue's employment records, then said to Mark and Corky, "I called Sergeant McGrath this morning and told him what had happened. He should have come by the fire site while you were there, Corky."

"I didn't see him," Corky replied.

The temporary clerk brought Sue's file into the office. Jeff found Sergeant McGrath's phone number and called it for the second time. McGrath was retired from the city police force and, as far as Jeff knew, was not working, yet there was no answer. Jeff left a message on the answering machine asking McGrath to return his call.

"Let's assume for the moment that Sue died in the fire," Mark said, "do we let the issue of the disks drop?"

"As far as the town attorney is concerned it is a non-issue, Mark. We covered that," Jeff said.

"Judy and I have a personal interest in those disks, Jeff," Mark said. "I'd like to take a look at the fire scene and see if there is any possibility that they are there."

"Contact the arson investigator, Mark. He's trained to look for evidence at a fire scene. Do you think for one moment that ZIP disks could withstand a fire of that intensity?"

"I don't know, Jeff, but I'll speak with the arson investigator. Who is he?" Mark asked.

"You'll have to ask the fire commander," Jeff answered. "He called for an investigation and will probably ask the Chicago Fire Department to lend a hand. Now for another matter. If it is Sue's body we will participate in her funeral no matter what you might suspect, Mark. She was a positive and productive employee in this department for a long time. Any objections?" Jeff asked, looking intently at Mark.

"None," Mark answered. Corky nodded.

"I'll let you both know what Dr. Spencer finds," Jeff said, standing. The others left the office.

At 3:00 P.M., a very husky voice called the police station asking for Captain Myers. "Who may I tell him is calling?" the temporary clerk asked.

"Marty McGrath," the voice answered. The clerk transferred the call to Captain Myers.

"Hello, Sergeant," Jeff greeted. "Have you been to the house?"

"You can drop the 'sergeant'," McGrath said. "That was a long time ago, but thanks for the courtesy. It's Marty. And yes, I've been to the house. I spoke with Dr. Spencer before he moved the body to the clinic."

After a long pause, Jeff said, "I know this is difficult for you, Marty, but we need to make a positive identification. Did you and Dr. Spencer speak about Sue's dentist?"

"No, but I can imagine why you need to know," McGrath replied. "She was a patient of Dr. Poyer."

"May I share that information with Dr. Spencer?" Jeff asked.

"Certainly," McGrath replied.

"Marty, I'll let you know the minute we have an identification," Jeff promised.

"It won't be a surprise, Jeff," McGrath replied. "I know it's Sue, but I'll wait for your call."

Drs. Spencer and Poyer met in the lobby of the clinic, and Spencer took him to the examination room. Both the impressions and the x-rays confirmed Sue McGrath's identity. Spencer thanked Poyer, then called Jeff Myers with their results.

"Were there injuries other than burning?" Jeff asked.

"Not that I can see," Spencer answered. "Do you plan to call Marty McGrath?"

"I'll take care of the rest of the notifications," Jeff answered. "You can call Marty later this afternoon when it's time for a funeral director to pick up the body."

Spencer agreed and got McGrath's number. As far as Spencer was concerned the death was the result of burning, and the victim was Susan McGrath. There was no evidence of other injury to the body. He would certify his findings.

Shortly after receiving information from Captain Myers that the body had been identified, Mark received a call from the RFD commander that a meeting was to be held at 4:00 P.M. in the department conference room. Mark arrived late, but withheld his apologies when he learned that the arson investigator had not yet arrived. The fire commander was a young man, barely thirty. There was seriousness in his eyes that belied his youth. He stood almost as tall as Mark and was broad shouldered. With the trace of a smile, he extended his hand to Mark and introduced himself. "Coffee?" he asked.

"Sounds good," Mark replied. They both walked to the coffee counter in the conference room. "Have you heard anything from the arson investigator?" Mark asked.

"Not yet. I'm hoping to get a report this afternoon. He requested the meeting," the man replied. Just as Mark and the fireman were taking seats at the conference table, the arson investigator entered.

"Good afternoon, gentlemen," he said with authority. After pulling a manila folder from his briefcase, he opened it and withdrew what appeared to be a typed report. Without any formal greeting, the investigator began to make his report. "Let me begin by saying that I have no reason to believe that there was arson involved in the house fire under investigation. We have spent two days combing through the fire site, and we have used one of our dogs at the site. The dog immediately responded to an exploded can found near the base of the water heater. Lab tests determined that the can had contained gasoline. Not far from the exploded can was a gasoline-powered lawn mower with an exploded fuel tank. The victim's body was found between the lawn mower and the water heater. It is our determination that the victim was handling gasoline near the water heater, and that fumes from the gasoline were ignited by the pilot light at the base of the water heater. The can containing gasoline apparently exploded creating an intense fire in the garage. The mishandling of the accelerant caused the fire and consequent death. I have ruled out arson." He closed his manila folder and began to place it back in his briefcase.

Mark asked, "Did Captain Myers speak to you about some ZIP disks of interest to the RPD?"

"Yes, he did," the investigator answered. "We did not find any ZIP disks. Are there any other questions?" Neither Mark nor the fireman had any questions. The investigator closed his briefcase and left the room, ending the meeting.

Susan McGrath was buried at Rest Haven Cemetery. Even though Mark and Sue had been friends for over a decade and worked closely together during that period, Mark could not suppress his suspicions about Sue's involvement in the matter of the Archer disks.

Mark turned his police vehicle towards the townhouse. The issue that had interrupted their honeymoon was now settled in his mind, and he looked forward to a fresh start with Judy.

Mark hadn't thought to get a key to the townhouse, so he rang the bell. He could hear Judy playing her guitar through the open upstairs bedroom window. Kelly yelped, the guitar stopped, and in seconds the door opened. Judy handed Mark the handle of the leash with Kelly snapped to the other end, and a plastic sandwich bag. "What's the bag for?" Mark asked.

"For scooping poop," Judy answered. "Welcome to city life."

"Do I get a kiss first?" Mark asked, trying to step through the door.

"Earn it," Judy said, smiling.

"And so it starts," Mark said to Kelly as they headed for the curb.

Duty done, Mark rang the bell again, then he and Kelly stepped inside. Mark was amazed that almost all of the boxes they had moved from the Tetlow's were gone. "You've been busy," he said.

"Got almost everything put away," Judy said as she slipped a key from a key ring and handed it to Mark. "Here's a key to the townhouse." She took Mark by the hand and led him to the love seat in the living room. Mark sat down and Judy retrieved a bottle of Sam Adam's Ale, Mark's favorite. She sat on the floor between his knees and rested her head on his leg. "How was your day?"

Mark told her about the fire investigation. She asked "What about the disks?"

"Probably destroyed in the fire, if she had them," Mark answered.

"Then that ends Bob's project," she said.

"The Arson Investigator looked for ZIP disks," Mark said, "but didn't find any. Even if he had, I doubt that they'd be useful."

Mark went into the bedroom and changed into Levi's and a buttoned short-sleeved shirt, and loafers. Judy, a quiz-show junkie, sat down in the front bedroom to watch Jeopardy. Kelly lay down at her feet. When Mark reentered, Judy was drinking a glass of water. There was only one chair in the bedroom, so Mark sat on the edge of the bed. "There are some things that we need to talk about, Judy," he said over the sound of the TV.

Judy got up, turned off the television, and said, "Could it wait until after dinner?"

"Sure," Mark agreed. He was looking at Judy as he spoke, but there was no recognition in her face. As she stared at him, the glass of wine slipped from her hand and fell on Kelly spilling wine on his coat. Almost as soon as it fell, Judy jolted back to reality.

"It happened again, didn't it?" she asked.

Mark was picking up the wineglass. "How often does this happen?" he asked.

"It's the second time today," she answered, tears forming in her eyes.

"I think it's time for you to be tested, Judy," Mark suggested.

"There's no need, Mark. I know what it is," she asserted.

"Are there any other symptoms?" he asked.

Without answering Judy stood and, staggering, nearly collapsed in Mark's arms. He led her to the bed where she lay down next to Mark. Rolling toward him, she lifted her head onto his chest. While Judy cried softly, Mark said, "Judy, it's time for you to see a doctor. Even if you aren't tested they can treat the symptoms." She agreed.

9

At the beginning of December, the Research Director reported to the Executive Committee of Bio-Gen, "We received written notice from the FDA yesterday, and we have approval for animal testing."

"Gentlemen," Aaron Krimer III began, "we were formed for one purpose—to help develop the Human Genome Project. Until now, as you know, we have been an important part of that program. Very soon, the laboratories licensed by NIH to develop the human genome will have achieved their goal. Mapping of the human genome is nearing completion, but there is still much work to do as we put our knowledge of the human genome to work to better the human condition. With the work Dr. Archer did on Gene 15105 we are a leg up on our competition. Granted, Archer did not have proper authority for the work that he did, but now that we have replicated his research we know that we can exploit it, both for the continued profitability of Bio-Gen and for the betterment of humanity. With the approval of the FDA to proceed with animal testing, I am prepared to recommend that we go full speed ahead with the development of 15105."

"What is the risk that Archer's protocol will come back to haunt us?" Rory Sanders asked.

"Little to none," Krimer answered. "There are only a few on our staff who know the full history of 15105, and I believe that we can trust their discretion. We will, of course, have to see that they are well treated. As far as the FDA is concerned the data we submitted was developed in our own labs. We alone know its origin. What we have done in our labs has been properly documented."

Adding to Krimer's answer, the Research Director said, "History is re-plete with stories of drugs whose research was done outside of normal protocol. In some cases, scientists have tested drugs on themselves before submitting them for approval. What Archer did was wrong, but not unique in the annals of science."

Frowning, Sanders said, "I don't give a hoot about history. I just want to know that we are not jeopardizing ourselves or our company in the process."

Krimer intervened. "Gentlemen, are we in agreement that we should proceed with 15105? Are there any who disagree?" No one responded. Looking at the Research Director, the CEO said, "In that case, let's pro-ceed with animal testing."

Doctors Palmer and Phillips were delighted to receive an unusually large bonus in their company Christmas cards.

"Would you like to spend your Christmas vacation in New Hampshire?" Mark asked as he and Judy were deciding how to decorate the townhouse for the holiday.

"I'd love it," she answered, "but the school will only be closed from December 24 to January 2. Does that give us enough time?"

"It will if we pour the coals to that new car of yours." Mark said. Judy had traded her Escort for a Ford Excursion. "Although I'll have to spend my entire bonus filling up the gas tank on that hog."

"Four-wheel drive will be useful in New Hampshire," Judy rebutted.

Christmas was special for Mark. His parents decorated the house, splurged on gifts, and had parties. It was the only time that relatives came to his house, but he remembered those times. He wondered how many Christ-mases he and Judy would have together. Mark was seeing changes in Judy. Occasionally, she would flare up over nothing, then become depressed over her behavior. It didn't happen often, and Mark had learned not to react. She also had some difficulty concentrating on the students' home-work assignments, reading the same theme paper several times. He knew from his discussions with Dr. Spencer that these were symptoms. Her sei-zures continued at the same pace, but her "staggering" was more apparent and more frequent. Mark wondered how long she would be able to teach and drive safely. She stubbornly refused testing and treatment, as if to will the disease gone.

In Judy's family, decorating the house for Christmas was a special day. The whole family participated and, when the work was done, the family had cookies and eggnog. She wanted to continue that tradition. Judy took Mark by the hand and led him into the kitchen. Seating him at the table, she put glasses and a dish of almond crescent cookies in front of him, then went into the living room and put a Christmas album on the CD player. Returning to the kitchen, she poured eggnog into the glasses. "Let's always remember these times, Mark," she said. "Christmas is a special time for me, and I want it to be a special time for us."

"What makes it special for you, Judy?"

"First, because it is the celebration of Jesus' birth. We need to be reminded of what God did for us at the first Christmas, and what he continues to do for us," she answered. "Second, because it is a time for being together as a family and sharing God's love."

Mark reached across the table and took Judy's hand in his. "I love you, Judy," he said. Judy stood up and walked to Mark's side of the table. She took him by the hand into the living room where they danced to Christmas music without speaking. Mark could feel Judy's warm tears on his neck.

Mark and Corky worked out their vacation schedules so that Mark got the time between Christmas and New Year's. On Christmas Eve day, with the Excursion packed, Kelly at the kennel, and Judy's new Christmas skis attached to the roof rack alongside Mark's, they headed for New Hampshire.

The Excursion pulled into the gravel parking area of their chalet at 10:15 A.M. on Christmas morning. Mark checked each room and was pleased that the tenants had left the place in good shape. The weather was cold and snowy, so Mark adjusted the thermostat and brought in wood for the fireplace while Judy unpacked luggage and checked the refrigerator. Judy found the phone book and asked, "Are you interested in going to church? It is Christmas."

"Don't you think that most of the services will be over by now?"

"I'm going to check," Judy said. She searched the yellow pages and found eight churches listed. Not caring which church she attended, she began with the first. It was a Methodist Church.

"Merry Christmas. Emmanuel United Methodist Church," the voice said.

"Merry Christmas," Judy replied, "are you having a Christmas service today?"

"We just finished the early service, and we'll be starting the late service at 11:00 A.M.," the person answered. "Can you join us?"

"We've just arrived from out of town, and we're in our traveling clothes," Judy said.

"We get lots of tourists here. Come as you are. We'd love to have you," the friendly voice replied.

"Thank you," Judy said, then got directions to the church and said goodbye. She walked through the snow to the woodshed. Mark was closing the door and had a stack of wood in his arms. "If we hurry, we can still make the late service at the Methodist Church!"

Emmanuel United Methodist Church was established in Woodsville in 1847 and was still occupying its original red brick building. A lighted sign with movable letters stood next to the sidewalk leading to the front door. Inside was a small Narthex with a guest book on a stand to the left and a glass-enclosed bulletin board on the wall to the right. An elderly gentleman greeted Mark and Judy, then handed each of them a service folder. They proceeded into the sanctuary and took a seat in a pew towards the rear. Above and behind them was a choir balcony. There were sounds of chairs shuffling and the murmur of voices, so Judy assumed that there would be choir music. When the prelude began the pews were almost filled. The prelude moved into the first hymn, *Oh, Come, All Ye Faithful*, everyone stood, and the acolyte and pastor processed from the rear. Judy was surprised that the pastor was a young woman. She was robed in white and had a white stole over her shoulders.

The pastor preached a short homily on the Christmas theme, and the rest of the service was mainly a celebration of songs shared between the congregation and the choir. During the closing hymn, *Joy to the World*, the acolyte and Pastor recessed to the rear of the church where she greeted worshipers on their way. She welcomed Judy and Mark to Emmanuel and invited them to return. Judy's first Christmas in New Hampshire was off to a great start.

Exhausted, Judy and Mark collapsed into bed when they returned to the chalet, but neither could sleep. Because she needed to be measured, Mark had already given Judy her Christmas presents—skis, boots, and accessories, but Judy would give no hint about what she had for Mark. Lying in bed exhausted but with her eyes wide open, she turned toward Mark. "Would you like to have your Christmas present?"

"Now?" Mark said sleepily.

"Are you going to be able to sleep?"

"Not with you talking."

"Okay. I'll just wait until you wake up."

"All right," he conceded, "let me have it."

"You have to get up and come with me."

"Where to?"

"Just follow me," Judy answered. She took him by the hand and led him to the screened porch. "Just wait here." She stepped out of the porch in her bare feet into the snow and disappeared around the side of the chalet.

"Where are you going half-naked?" Mark called after her. Before she could answer she reappeared dragging a new bike through the snow and into the porch. Mark helped her with the bike and said, "You are a crazy woman."

"This is to replace your old Schwinn," she said, remembering their first bike ride at Riverside Park. She had bought a Gary Fisher Sugar-1 in Amarillo yellow to match hers. Merry Christmas!

Donna Kraft grew up in Crofton, Maryland, and graduated from Wesley Theological Seminary in Washington D.C. after earning her undergraduate degree at the University of Maryland in College Park. She was ordained at her home church in Crofton and installed as Pastor of Emmanuel United

Methodist Church in Woodsville at the age of twenty-seven where she had served for three years. She felt blessed to have been given the assignment to the Woodsville church because her husband, David, a ranger with the United States Forest Service, worked on the New Hampshire stretch of the Appalachian Trail. The church still owned a parsonage and maintained it well, which was satisfactory as long as the Kraft's had no children, but they knew that they would have to make other housing arrangements when children came.

Tanned and trim, Donna stood five feet, three inches and weighed ninety-eight pounds. Her shoulder-length brown hair was combed in a page boy style. She wore contact lenses over her brown eyes, and had a flawless complexion. An athlete and accomplished skier, Donna had to force herself to stick to her work schedule on days like this one. With the Advent and Christmas season now past, the sun gleaming through the trees, and seven inches of fresh snow on the slopes, it was impossible for her to sit at the desk in her small parsonage office. She debated whether to answer the phone when it rang. Duty prevailed.

"Hello, this is Judy Garrison. My husband, Mark, and I attended your late service yesterday. I was wondering whether I might stop by your office today."

"I was just getting ready to leave, Judy. Is this an emergency?"

"No, but I'll only be here for a few days and I'd like to speak with you if you can make time."

"Would you like to take a walk with me. I need to get out of the office," Donna said, not thrilled about walking on a perfect ski day.

"Could I come in about thirty minutes?" Judy asked.

"Thirty minutes it is."

"Who was on the phone?" Mark asked.

"The Pastor from Emmanuel."

"Did she call for a reason?"

"Actually, I called her, Mark."

"Really? Why?"

"I need to talk to a pastor," Judy said.

Mark didn't know where the conversation was going. He sensed that this was important to Judy and he didn't want to probe.

"What about our plans for today?" Mark asked.

"I'll only be gone for an hour or so," Judy promised. "We're going to take a walk as soon as I can get there. I should be back by ten."

"Have fun," Mark said without enthusiasm.

Emmanuel's parsonage was about 200 yards south of the church. Donna was sitting on a step leading to the front door. A sandy-haired man was sitting next to her. Dressed in a brown quilted one-piece work garment that zipped from his collar to his crotch, he seemed bigger than he probably was. His face was already becoming weathered from exposure to the out-doors, and his hair was tousled as he removed his leather, ear-muffed cap that read "Woodsville" above the bill. He stood as Judy approached, re-moved a glove from his right hand, then extended it to Judy. "Dave Kraft," he said. Judy shook his hand and introduced herself. "I'll see you later, honey," he said to Donna, bending down to kiss her, then disappeared to the rear of the parsonage.

"Dave is splitting wood today," Donna said. "He's got the week off. He's a Forest Service Ranger who works the New Hampshire stretch of the Appalachian Trail. Not only was he born to this work, but also he's native to New Hampshire. Would you like a cup of coffee before we start our walk?"

"No thanks, Pastor. Mark and I have plans today and I promised I wouldn't be gone long."

"Please call me Donna. That answers another question. We'll take the short route," Donna pointed out places of interest along the way. At the corner of Ammonoosuc and Nelson Streets they rested on a wrought iron bench next to an historic plaque. "You said that you wanted to discuss something with me," Donna said, shifting to face Judy.

"Yes. I'm not proud of what I'm going to tell you, Donna," Judy be-gan. She explained her family's history with Huntington's Disease and her suspicions about her own condition, then told of how she had kept this information from Mark until after they were married. When she was fin-ished, she was surprised at how easy it had been to tell these things to Donna.

"Have you asked for his forgiveness?" Donna asked.

"Yes, and he has said that he forgives me."

"But you haven't forgiven yourself," Donna said, more as a statement than a question.

"That's why I'm here."

"Have you asked for God's forgiveness?"

"Yes."

"Then what are you asking of me?" Donna said. Her question surprised Judy.

"I'm not sure," Judy said. "I guess I just needed to tell someone."

"Do you want me to speak for God?" Donna asked.

"Perhaps."

"Okay. When you confessed to God that you married Mark under false pretenses, God heard you. Do you believe that?" Donna persisted.

"Yes, I believe that God hears our prayers," Judy answered.

"And our prayers of confession," Donna added. "And he forgives us, and more than that. He promises to put our sins as far from us as the East is from the West. God forgives, and then does something that we aren't able to do—he forgets."

"I wish that I could forget," Judy said.

"You're human," Donna said. "It's probably something that you'll never forget, but God has forgiven you, Judy, and Mark has forgiven you. Your job is to get on with your marriage and your life. If you cling to your guilt, you will hurt no one but yourself."

"I ask God's forgiveness every day for what I've done," Judy said.

"Then you are insulting God," Donna said. "It's as if you are telling him that his forgiveness isn't sincere, as if he didn't get it right the first time. God forgave you from the first time that you confessed, then promptly forgot what you confessed. When you keep coming back to him you cast doubt on his sincerity."

Judy sat silently, considering what Donna had said. After a moment, she began to cry as if a tremendous weight had been lifted from her. Donna reached out to Judy and held her as she sobbed. Then, as quickly as the tears had come, they stopped. Judy sat upright and said, "Thank you."

"Shall we get you back to Mark?" Donna asked, standing.

"Yes," Judy answered. They reversed course and returned to the parsonage. Donna respected Judy's thoughts and little was said. When they reached the parsonage, Judy said goodbye on the road.

"I know that you and Mark are on vacation and only have a few days, but would you like to have dinner with Dave and me while you're here? Perhaps we could get better acquainted."

"I'd like that very much," Judy said.

"Dave and I love to ski. He's an instructor."

"Just what I need. Can I call you after I talk to Mark?"

"Leave a message on the church machine if we don't answer," Donna said, waving goodbye.

It was 9:00 A.M. when Judy returned to the chalet. Mark was setting out their ski equipment. "How did it go with the Pastor?" he asked.

"I like her very much," Judy answered. "Donna asked whether we'd like to have dinner with them."

"Tonight?" Mark asked.

"Whenever," Judy answered. "They like to ski. David is an instructor."

Mark looked forward to teaching Judy how to ski. "Why don't we go on the community slope today?"

"Great!" Judy replied. "I'll call her now, then we can go."

The community slope with its one trail was packed. The snow was perfect, and the sun was shining through the trees. They parked their Excursion in the parking lot and walked the short distance to the ski cabin. Here they had made love, and here Mark had learned Judy's secret, but now they were intent on enjoying this moment. "Is there a bunny slope, Mark?" Judy asked.

"Not a formal training slope, Judy, but there is a small hill on the other side of the parking lot for beginners. Would you like to go there?" Judy nodded.

Turning around before they reached the cabin, they returned to the parking lot. Passing through the lot Judy saw a small sloped roof that appeared to be sticking out of the ground. As they walked to the front of the roof, she saw that it was a covered bench much like a baseball dugout. "Will I be the only adult learning how to ski?" Judy asked.

"In New Hampshire children learn to walk and ski at about the same time," Mark said, smiling. "Not to worry. The worst that can happen is that people will point and laugh."

"Thanks," Judy said as they found places on the long bench.

Athletic by nature, Judy learned quickly, falling only several times. Each time Mark skied easily to her rescue. In an hour she felt ready to try the slope. The ski cabin was crowded with people donning or shedding equipment. A fire was roaring in the wood stove. It was just as Judy imagined a ski cabin should be. Just outside the cabin a line was formed at the lift. They took their place in the line and were soon hoisted to the top of the slope. Leery of heights, it took Judy only a few minutes to adjust to the lift. She was stunned by what she could see. From her lift chair she could see the River and much of the town of Woodsville. Too soon, the lift slowed and she and Mark were on the ground ready for her first terrifying slide to the bottom. It was a small slope when compared with the commercial slopes nearby, but Judy felt as though she was on the top of Mt. Everest. She couldn't imagine herself skiing to the bottom. Amazingly, she did it without mishap on the first try. She was hooked, and Mark was delighted. "You're a natural," he said proudly. By the end of the afternoon Judy had fallen twice without injury on six runs down the slope. They returned to the chalet by way of the Supermarket.

"I really like the Kraft's," Mark said as he entered the chalet.

"I do, too," she responded. "How would you feel about skiing with them tomorrow?" Both were a little muscle-sore from their first day on the slope, but they wanted to see the Kraft's again, so Mark agreed. "Do you think it would be too late to call them," Judy asked.

"It's only been fifteen minutes since I dropped them off," Mark said. Donna answered the phone and eagerly accepted the invitation. They agreed to meet at 11:00 A.M. at the community slope.

The next day was cloudy. Snow was predicted for midday with the possibility of heavy accumulation. By 11:15 they had made two runs without incident when the snow began to come down. It came down lightly at first so they rode the lift to the top for a third run. Dave was first off, followed by Donna, then Judy. Mark brought up the rear. Judy failed to negotiate a dog leg turn near the bottom of the slope and fell, sliding into the trunk of a tree. Mark reached her quickly and helped her back onto her skis. There was a slight bump on the right of her forehead and a bleeding cut about one half inch long. It wasn't deep, but was bleeding enough to require stitches. With Mark's handkerchief tied around Judy's head, they made their way slowly to the bottom of the slope. At the ski cabin the attendant dressed Judy's wound.

"You need to have that stitched," Donna insisted. The attendant agreed.

"Is there a hospital in Woodsville?" Judy asked.

"We can go to our doctor," Donna offered. "You'll like her." In a matter of minutes, they were in the Excursion headed for Woodsville. Even though the snow was falling heavily, the Excursion had no trouble negotiating the road.

Donna was right. Judy liked Dr. Ryan. Without any front office formalities, the doctor took Judy to her treatment room, cleaned the wound, and then closed it with two stitches. "How did this happen?" the doctor asked.

"I fell skiing," Judy answered.

"Novice?" the doctor asked, smiling.

"Learned yesterday," Judy replied.

"Be careful, Judy," the doctor suggested. "I don't do broken bones."

"Trust me," Judy said. Judy knew that the fall had nothing to do with her skill as a skier. She had no recollection of falling and didn't regain awareness until Mark was helping her to her feet. She knew it was the last time that she would ever ski. In less than fifteen minutes, Judy was checking out. "What kind of doctor is she?" Judy asked Donna.

"She has a family practice," Donna answered. "We've been seeing her since she opened her office about three years ago. We think she's great."

Judy picked up a business card at the front desk as they were leaving the office.

Mark drove the Kraft's to the parsonage. As he and Judy were pulling away, Judy said, "I had a seizure on the slope."

"Is that why you fell?"

"Yes, I blacked out. One moment I was skiing, then you were helping me up. It would have been worse if I had been at the top of the hill. I don't think that I should ski again."

"Why not discuss this with Dr. Spencer when we return home?" Mark asked. "He may be able to prescribe something that will prevent the seizures." After a pause, Judy agreed.

10
Five years later

Mark lay on his side looking at Judy. She is as beautiful as the day I met her, he thought. Judy was sleeping, the only time that her body was completely at rest. Her blonde hair was cut short now to make it easier to brush, but her eyes were the same—deep blue and full of life. Mark worried about her weight loss. Dr. Spencer insisted that she exercise regularly to slow down her symptoms, but that escalated the weight loss.

Mark hoped that Judy would like the surprise he planned for their fifth anniversary. Five years, he thought, and how fast it had gone. How many more, he wondered. Getting up quietly so as not to wake Judy, he went downstairs to the kitchen telephone and dialed Becky Malott. What would he do without Becky—Judy's best friend, teaching colleague, maid of honor, and now, caregiver? Every day during the summer Becky came to the townhouse to check on Judy. Mark didn't know what would happen when school started in several weeks. "Hello," Becky said.

"Hi, Becky, it's Mark. I'm sorry to call so early, but I wanted you to know that I've taken the day off to be with Judy. It's our fifth anniversary. I'll let you know if I get called in, but for now you don't need to come by."

"I know it's your anniversary. I was there, remember? Have a happy anniversary, and tell Judy that I'll see her tomorrow."

"You're a doll," Mark said as he hung up the telephone. He went back upstairs and lay down next to Judy. Just as he dozed, Judy stirred and flopped her arm onto his chest. She hated to wake up, never knowing what the day held in store. Mark didn't expect her to remember the anniversary, but she surprised him.

"Happy anniversary, honey," she said, then moved closer to him and laid her head on his shoulder.

"Happy anniversary," Mark replied. "I'm going to stay home today for the occasion." He didn't tell her about the surprise he had planned.

"Oh, good," she said and kissed him on his neck. "I've been lying here thinking about what I should do when school starts."

"What have you decided?" Mark asked.

"I think that I'm going to quit teaching," she said. Mark wasn't surprised or disappointed. They didn't need her salary to get by, and it was getting more difficult for her to teach.

Mark sat up at the side of the bed. "This is a day for celebration!" He got up and headed for the door. "I'll be right back," he said as he left the room. Judy hoped that he wasn't going to bring her breakfast in bed. She didn't think that she could fake her way through more runny eggs and burnt bacon. She was relieved when Mark returned with an envelope in his hands. "Happy anniversary," he said, handing her the envelope.

"This isn't fair," she said. "I won't open this until I get your card." She got up from the bed and nearly fell to the floor. Mark didn't respond. She did not allow him to help her when she lost her balance. Recovering, she walked unsteadily to the dresser, removed a card from the top drawer, then handed it to Mark. Mark was impressed. He doubted that she'd remember their anniversary. "Becky and I shopped for this yesterday," she said. Of course, Mark thought, Becky remembered.

"Who first?" Mark asked.

"You first," Judy answered. It was the first mushy card she had ever given Mark. They usually traded humorous cards. He read the verse, "For all our days and all our nights, you'll have all my love. Happy Anniversary." As much as he tried not to, he couldn't help but wonder how many days and nights that would be.

"Thank you, and you shall have all of mine," he promised. "Now, it's your turn."

Judy opened the envelope and removed the card. It was a Garfield card with a humorous verse. She smiled, then opened a smaller envelope that was tucked inside the card. It was a printed announcement from Festival Cruise Lines that reservations for a Caribbean cruise had been made for Lieutenant and Mrs. Mark Garrison for seven days beginning on May 20. She didn't move. Her eyes remained fixed on the card.

"Judy?" Mark asked.

"I'm okay," Judy said, "I just can't believe this. We've never been on a cruise."

"Then it's about time, wouldn't you say?" Mark asked.

"Can we afford this?" Judy asked.

"That's not a question you ask when someone gives you a gift," Mark quipped.

"I love you so much, Mark," Judy said, taking his hand in hers.

"We've got some planning to do between now and May," Mark said.

"The first thing that I'm going to do is email Donna," Judy said. "She and Dave have been on a cruise to Alaska. She'll know exactly what it's like."

The phone rang while George was shaving. He put down his shaver, walked into the bedroom and answered. It was a wrong number. It struck George that he was no longer apprehensive when the phone rang. It had been over five years since the last call from the blackmailer. He was certain that the caller was a woman, but he also knew that a man's voice could be made to sound like a woman's with the help of a voice scrambler. Whoever it was, there had been no further contact, which undoubtedly meant that no copies of Archer's disks had been kept. Perhaps there was honor among thieves.

Bio-Gen was at a critical stage in the research of the 15105 correction. As Project Director in the Research Department it was up to George and his assistant, Dr. Michele Phillips, to shepherd the project to the next stage, human testing. The Executive Committee had established close boundaries around the project. Only a handful of research scientists were assigned to 15105 for security reasons, and the test results were considered top secret. It was unofficially called the Aspirin Project because of the widespread benefits that were being seen in animal testing, the easy availability of ingredients, and the low cost of production.

Animal testing had yielded amazing results. In George's latest summary report to the Executive Committee he noted the wide range of effects. Excesses of all kinds were modified in every species tested. Aggressive behavior was pacified, lethargic behavior became more attentive, and physical maladies of every sort were cured. Five years of testing had yielded consistent results. No side effects of any kind had been reported. Month after month George submitted the same findings. The only variation in the testing had been the species of animal life being tested.

George could foresee a dilemma. If human testing yielded the same amazing results, how would the product be marketed? And would Bio-Gen get patent protection? Would the government allow them to charge enough to recoup their research costs, or would they insist that the product be available in large quantities at low cost? One result of animal testing was certain—the biological half-life of the product was two days meaning that the product had to be taken daily, and if missed for as little as one week the animals regressed to their former state. The profit potential for this product was unbelievable, and unless the government mandated otherwise, Bio-Gen had it sewn up, at least until the hoped-for patent expired.

To the best of George's recollection, no product had had the wide range of effect on animal life as this genetic remedy. Bob Archer had developed what could become the most important health product ever. Human testing would take a period of years, but George, Michele, and the Executive Committee were aware of Dr. Archer's clandestine human tests and the results. Their confidence level was already high.

Judy spent hours preparing herself for their anniversary dinner. The occasional spasmodic movements of her arms and head made it difficult for her to apply her makeup, but she did it without help. Mark snapped her necklace and zipped her dress. She was ravishing, he thought, and he wanted to make love to her on this anniversary night.

"Mark, I have a confession to make," Judy said as Mark sipped a vodka martini. The medications that Dr. Spencer prescribed for Judy conflicted with alcohol, so she was resigned to a glass of Sprite. They had a well-placed table near the window nineteen stories above Lake Michigan. Although the table was not isolated, there was no one at the adjoining table, and Mark hoped that his encouragement to the maitre d' was enough to keep it that way until they were finished.

"Confess away," Mark said, thinking that she had entertained some lustful fantasy.

"I've thought about killing myself," she said. Mark stared in disbelief. He didn't know how to respond. "I'm sorry to say this now, but it has been on my mind and I've been afraid to tell you.

"As I get worse, I think more and more about my father," she said. "Before they took him away, I could hear him downstairs. It was awful. No one should have to go through this."

"But he didn't kill himself," Mark said.

"He didn't succeed," she corrected. Mark was surprised. No one had ever said that Richard Hammond had tried to commit suicide. "I believe that he tried."

"Why do you say that?" Mark asked.

"Because one night I heard my mother yell, 'Richard, why have you done this?' Then the ambulance came and took my father. He never came home again. He died a year and a half later in a nursing home."

"Did you ask your mother what had happened?" Mark asked.

"No, I don't think she would have told me," Judy answered. "She tried to protect me from all of that."

"Judy, I don't know what to say. You scare me when you talk like this. I can't be with you every moment to protect you from yourself. I can only tell you that I love you and I want what's best for you, and I don't think that killing yourself is the answer."

"This is only the beginning, Mark. This could go on for many years. It took my father ten years to die, but some Huntington patients live for twenty years, or more. I couldn't take that. My symptoms are bearable now, but they will get worse—a lot worse before the end."

"I'm not in your place, Judy. I don't know what to say now. I need time to think. Promise me that you won't do anything until we've had time to work this out," Mark pleaded.

"I will," she promised. "I'm sorry, Mark, that I spoiled our anniversary dinner. Can we salvage the night?"

"Starting this minute," Mark said. He motioned to the waiter. "You can't drink alcohol, but Dr. Spencer said nothing about eating lobster." Mark knew that this was Judy's favorite meal. They spent the rest of the evening wearing bibs bearing pictures of lobsters, cracking shells, dipping lobster in melted butter, and sipping wine. When the meal was over, Mark drove them along the Outer Drive where they watched the waves under a star-studded sky. He parked the Excursion at the end of a beach parking lot, and they necked like high schoolers. After an hour or so, they returned home.

Mark helped Judy unzip her dress, then let the dress fall to the floor, and removed the rest of her clothes. She fell back on the bed naked and motioned for Mark to join her. He didn't need a second invitation. It felt good to be in the bed they still shared. They were both grateful that her symptoms were at rest during sleep. It had become the best time for both of them. He could imagine Judy without Huntington's as she lay quietly asleep. For now, she didn't choose to sleep. She still had a normal sexual appetite and her disease did not get in the way. Taking the necessary precautions, they made passionate love, then fell asleep in each other's arms.

"Hello, Lois," Mark said when Judy's mother answered the phone. "Do you have a few minutes to talk?"

"Yes, of course, Mark. Is everything all right?" Lois asked.

"I think so, but Judy said something at dinner last night that I need to clarify with you," Mark said.

"By the way, happy anniversary," Lois interrupted.

"Thanks, and thanks for the card," Mark replied.

"What did Judy say?"

"She said that Richard attempted suicide. Is that correct?" Mark asked, not sure what kind of response to expect. There was a pause before Lois spoke. Mark let it happen.

"I'm surprised that Judy knew that. We never discussed it," Lois said.

"Then it's true?"

"Yes, it's true," Lois said. "Huntington's patients go through a lot. It's very difficult. Each day is a nightmare, especially towards the end. Richard had had enough, I guess, and he knew what it was doing to Judy and me."

"I know that Huntington's patients are prone to suicide," Mark said. "What did Richard do?"

"I was out for a short while, shopping for groceries, I think," Lois said. "When I returned his breathing was very labored and his eyes were closed. I couldn't wake him up. His medicine bottles were scattered. He had tried to open as many as he could, which was difficult for him, and he had swallowed some. Fortunately, swallowing was also very difficult for him, and we don't think that he took many. There were bottles and spilled pills everywhere. Anyway, I called the doctor and he sent an ambulance. In those days, anyone who attempted suicide had to be under observation for awhile. We found a nice nursing home where he remained until he died a year and a half later. After what he went through in that last year and a half, I'm not sure that I did the right thing by calling the doctor."

"Are you saying that suicide might have been better than what he experienced? How could you have lived with that?" Mark asked.

"Someday I will tell you about that last year and a half," Lois said. "You don't need to hear about it now, nor does Judy."

Mark was distracted at work. Everyone at the station knew that Judy was sick and made allowances for Mark's occasional lapses of attention. Captain Myers encouraged Mark to take whatever time he needed to care of Judy. After speaking with Lois, Mark needed to go home, but first he made arrangements to meet Dr. Spencer at Marge's Diner.

As he parallel parked in front of the diner he could see Dr. Spencer in a booth. He had changed. He was older, thinner, and, it seemed, even shorter. "Hi," Mark said as he slid into the booth across from the doctor.

"Hi, Mark," Spencer said, "How's Judy."

"Same as when you saw her last month, I suppose," Mark answered. "But she said something that has concerned me. At our anniversary dinner she said that she had thought of killing herself."

"I believe I mentioned that possibility when we first spoke about Huntington's," Spencer said.

"Yes, you did, and I remember that," Mark said, "but she caught me off guard. I didn't think that she was at that point."

"She probably isn't, Mark, but she has seen what the disease did to her father," Spencer said. "Unless you have seen it up close you can't imagine how devastating it is. And today we have ways of treating the symptoms that weren't available to Judy's father."

"Do you think that you can treat Judy's anxiety?" Mark asked.

"I'd say she is probably experiencing depression, Mark," Spencer said, "and, yes, we can treat the depression, but Judy has refused to take what I prescribed. I believe Prozac might be of help, but she has to agree to take it."

"Dr. Spencer," Mark started out thoughtfully, "how can I prevent her from taking her own life?"

"You can't, Mark," Spencer said firmly. "However, there will come a time when she will be unable to do it without help because she won't be able to coordinate her hands or swallow effectively."

"Where do you stand on the issue of assisted suicide?" Mark asked. Spencer paused.

"I'm a doctor, Mark. My life has been devoted to delaying death, not assisting it. And I'm a Roman Catholic with strong religious views about the value of life. You should know that not many people die in agonizing pain anymore, Mark. We can treat most pain, but diseases like Huntington's are different. Like Hanson's disease, or leprosy as it is commonly called, there isn't always a great deal of pain. Death usually occurs from infection, injuries from a fall, or other complications. Huntington's is a disease of the brain in which certain nerve cells waste away. As a result, Judy is already experiencing uncontrolled movements and brain disturbances, such as seizures. This will continue. I know that these things are hard to hear, Mark, but this is what she is facing. Death might seem like a way to avoid the worst of Huntington's, but my convictions are such that death must come in God's time. I cannot assist Judy, and I don't think that's what you're asking."

"I'm not asking for that, Dr. Spencer, and you've answered my question," Mark responded. "I'm just frightened and frustrated. I can't be with her every minute, and neither can Becky, her friend, who will be going back to work when school starts."

"I know Becky. She brings Judy to my office. Judy is blessed to have such a friend. I wouldn't worry about Judy spending some time alone right now, but a time will come, perhaps in a year or so, when she will need a full-time companion. She should not be driving or taking any risks even now, Mark."

Mark looked at Dr. Spencer. This man who had given so much to the people of Riverside looked old and tired. Even so, he had done his home-work on Huntington's, and Mark was grateful. "Is it asking too much for you to continue seeing Judy, Dr. Spencer?"

"I'm glad that you asked that, Mark, and I'm going to answer you honestly. I am not seeing any patients except Judy, and I have given up my part-time work as coroner. It might be better for you to find a doctor closer to where you live. I would suggest a doctor who has some experi-ence with Huntington's. I can make a referral if you wish."

Mark suspected that this might be the last time that he would see Dr. Spencer. With Ed dead, Marge retired, and Dr. Spencer retiring from his practice, Mark felt as though his past was slipping away from him. He finished his iced tea, thanked Dr. Spencer and accepted his offer for a referral, then stood to shake hands. Spencer slid out of the booth and slowly stepped forward to face Mark. His eyes were watering. Mark was not a hugger, but there in the aisle of Marge's Diner he broke his rule and wrapped his big arms around the frail, white-haired man, holding on to Dr. Spencer as if by doing so he could prevent the avalanche of his own history. Feelings thawing.

Mark left Marge's and drove home. Kelly was too old to greet anyone with more than a wag, so Mark bent down to him and scratched him behind his ears. Judy was at the kitchen table eating clam chowder. Her lower face was smeared with soup. Embarrassed to have Mark see her, she quickly wiped her face with a napkin. Mark didn't wish to risk her wrath by saying anything, so they both let the moment pass. A time would come when she would need to be fed, but this wasn't it. "Did you talk to Jeff about the holidays?" Judy asked.

"Yes, I did," Mark answered. "He has me scheduled to work Christ-mas. We'll have to go to New Hampshire at another time."

Judy was disappointed, but knew that Mark had been given more than his share of Christmases. "Since I'm not teaching, could you get away over Thanksgiving—perhaps from Wednesday night through the weekend?"

"If we drive straight through that will only allow two days to visit. I'll ask for a week, but first you had better email the Kraft's to make sure that they don't have other plans," Mark suggested. "It may be too early for skiing, and it will be too late for the fall colors." Mark wasn't ready to tell Judy that driving straight through was no longer an option. He couldn't drive for twenty-two hours without relief, and Judy couldn't relieve him. She didn't receive bad news well anymore, and Dr. Spencer's suggestion that she not drive was going to be bad news.

"Mark, I don't think that I'll ever ski again. The tranquilizer I'm taking has helped control my jerking, but as you saw on my face it doesn't do the whole job. That shouldn't stop you from skiing. I'll sit outside the cabin and watch you go by. That will be all right with me," Judy lied.

"Let's take one thing at a time," Mark suggested.

Judy was sitting in the living room when Mark brought the last of the luggage from the basement. "I've laid our clothes on the bed," she said. "When you get the luggage upstairs, I'll come up and help you pack."

"There's something I want to tell you, Judy," Mark began. "Something that Dr. Spencer said." He had already told her most of what Dr. Spencer had said. She knew that they would be seeing another doctor. She raised her eyebrows in anticipation and waited for Mark to speak. "He thinks that it is time for you to give up driving." Judy did not receive bad news well. He waited for the bomb to drop, but it didn't.

"I know that, Mark," Judy said quietly. "I don't trust myself to do a lot of things anymore. My life is slipping away." She began to cry. This was a reaction that Mark hadn't expected.

Trying to console her, he said, "There are still things that we can do together, honey. You still have your life. Please don't give up. I need you more than you can imagine, and if we can do nothing other than hold hands, that's enough for me."

"Just try holding my hand, Mark," Judy said. "If you can hold it still, you are better than I am." Then she laughed. "Now, let's not get morose.

Let's get on the road and have a nice Thanksgiving vacation. And I want to start with a glass of white Port no matter what it does to me!" They carried the luggage and wineglasses to their bedroom, then packed for the trip.

It took two days to get to Woodsville. Mark drove the whole way, but they napped at a rest area. Arriving in Woodsville on Sunday night, they found a note tacked to the front doorframe that read, "Gone with Dave. Back late Monday night, Donna." They would have the whole day Monday to get unpacked and rest from the trip. "This is the sixth year that we've come here, Mark," Judy said. "It's starting to feel like home." Mark felt the same way.

"Have you ever thought of moving here permanently?" Judy asked. Mark was surprised at her question.

"I've worked for seventeen years at the Riverside Police Department, Judy. My retirement is a long way off," he replied.

"I know, Mark," Judy said. "It was just a question."

Judy was sleeping when Donna knocked at the front door on Tuesday morning. Mark opened the door and placed his forefinger in front of his lips. She stepped in quietly and they hugged. "Where's Dave?" he asked.

"Working today," Donna answered. "He'll be off Wednesday through Friday."

"Great," Mark answered. He led Donna to the kitchen where he poured a mug of coffee for each of them, then they moved to the screened-in porch. The leaves were off of the trees and the weather was cool. The only sign of winter was the overcast sky. "I'm not going to awaken Judy," he said. "It's the only time that her body is fully at rest, and she needs to sleep."

"How is she doing, Mark?" Donna asked.

"She's progressing as expected," Mark answered.

"How close are the researchers to finding a cure?" Donna asked.

"Closing in," Mark replied. "They have isolated the defective gene which gives them a heads up on testing before symptoms develop. For now there is no cure, but who knows? Miracles happen."

"Does she still have mood swings? Last Christmas she bit my head off a few times over nothing, then felt terrible," Donna said.

"Yes, but that goes with the territory. If I have something to say that will set her off, I try to time it right. She can't help it, Donna. She's lucky to have you for a friend because you understand."

"All I know about Huntington's is what you and Judy have told me. Perhaps this is an insensitive question," Donna started. Mark cut her off.

"How long will she live?" he asked, finishing her question for her.

"Thanks, yes."

"It depends on how long the disease has been active. Symptoms may have started earlier than we realize, but were discounted. Usually death comes as early as ten years for adults, but it can be as long as twenty years, or even longer. Judy's symptoms are progressing fairly rapidly, and one of her symptoms has me worried, Donna."

"What's that?" Donna asked.

"She has spoken of suicide," Mark answered. Donna's eyes widened, and she shifted her position to face Mark squarely, inviting him with her eyes to continue.

"How often does she bring this up?" Donna asked.

"She's spoken of it several times," Mark answered, "and she knows that it is wrong in the eyes of God. I think that this is why her church life has slackened."

"Can I respond to that, Mark?" Donna asked not wanting to preach but feeling the need to clarify the teachings of Scripture.

"I wish you would," Mark said. "I'm conflicted about this. Judy has seen the devastation of Huntington's up close, and she knows what to expect. It scares her. I don't want her to suffer either, but the thought of taking one's life goes against everything I do and believe."

"Has she asked you to help her?" Donna asked.

"No. I hope she doesn't do that."

"Mark, the Bible teaches that life belongs to God. He gives it and He takes it on his own terms," Donna began. "'There is one passage in the Psalms that I have read to people who are at the end of life and want it over. Do you have your Bible close by?" Quietly, Mark got the Bible from the bedroom where Judy was sleeping. Donna flipped the pages to Psalm 139. "Here's what it says, '*When I was woven together in the depths of the earth, your eyes saw my unformed body. All the days ordained for me were written in your book before one of them came to be.*' I believe that this passage says all that we need to know about taking life, whether unborn life or life under stress. There are other places in the Bible where God lays claim to our lives. They do not belong to us, and we do not have the authority to take them."

"But why would God allow anyone to live with Huntington's?" Mark asked.

"God didn't invent disease, Mark," Donna answered. "Disease is part of the fallen nature of humankind. God heals disease, sometimes in this life, and always in the next—at least for those who trust Him, and I know that you and Judy trust Him. And God doesn't leave us alone in our suffering. In the first twelve verses of Psalm 139 King David speaks of the powerful presence of God in our lives."

"But that doesn't answer the question. Why does He let anyone suffer?"

"That is probably the question that pastors hear the most," Donna replied, "and I don't have the answer. I have seen many instances where suffering people have clung tenaciously to their faith right up to the end, and their courage and faithfulness have been God's way of bringing others to faith. And I have seen bridges built between warring factions in a family as they minister to someone dying a slow death. I'm sure that God has other reasons for what He does. One thing I do know, Mark, is that even though we don't have the answers now, we will have them eventually. Paul promises that someday we will know Him, that is God, as he now knows us. I look forward to that day."

"I hope that I will have the strength to live by your convictions when the situation gets worse, Donna," Mark said. "I haven't heard the last of this from Judy, I'm sure."

"Would you like for me to speak about this with her?"

"Only if she brings it up. Let's not wake a snake to kill it," Mark said, regretting his choice of words. "Hopefully she will come to her own understanding of God's will for her life and won't speak of suicide again." As he spoke they could hear Judy stirring in the bedroom. Donna put her hand on Mark's and squeezed it. At that moment Judy came into the kitchen.

"What's going on behind my back?" she asked, smiling. "Have I caught you two holding hands?"

"That's what happens when you sleep in," Donna said, hurrying to Judy and throwing her arms around her in a hug. The three played cards and games until Donna had to return to the parsonage to prepare dinner.

11

The main item on the agenda of the monthly operations meeting at Bio-Gen was Project 15105. Rory Sanders shepherded the meeting through all other business, dismissed all participants not directly involved with Project 15105, then called on Dr. George Palmer. "George, bring us up to speed on the Aspirin Project."

Remaining seated at his place at the conference table, George called on the other six people present to give status reports. In addition to Sanders, they were Dr. Michele Phillips and the directors of Animal Research, Purchasing, Cost Management, and Legal Services.

Animal Research reported continued good results. Purchasing reported that two pharmaceutical manufacturers had been queried on the product and were capable of producing the liposome-type product. Bids from both were acceptable to Purchasing and Cost Management. Legal Services reported that human testing could proceed as soon as product disclaimers and patient selection procedures were finalized. George was pleased with the reports. He then turned to Dr. Phillips who was coordinating the transition from animal to human testing. "Michele, what is the best date you can give for the beginning of human testing?"

"Approximately three months," Michele answered.

"Does anyone have any reason to challenge this?" George asked, surveying the room with his eyes. No one objected to Michele's projection. "Good. Then let's make sure it happens." George sat down.

"George, remain for a moment, please," Sanders said, then dismissed the others. When everyone had left, the COO looked intently at George. "I don't need to remind you, George, that you, Dr. Phillips, and the Executive

Committee are the only people who know how this product was developed, and that some human testing has already been conducted. I will remind you, however, that should this ever become generally known it could have serious consequences for you and for this company. Continue to be discreet, George. This product has the potential to be the wonder drug of this century. Let's not do anything to jeopardize that. Do we understand each other?"

George was surprised at the timing of the admonition. He had been warned before, but thought that he had earned the confidence of the Executive Committee. Perhaps they were just realizing the potential of the project and were nervous about the disclosure of Dr. Archer's work. "Yes, I understand fully," he answered. Sanders stood and left the room, leaving George behind.

On Wednesday the skies were overcast and the temperature was dropping. Mark woke up before Judy, dressed, and energized Mr. Coffee before moving firewood from the shed to the log holder outside the porch screen door. He carried some of the logs into the living room, loaded the fireplace insert, and started a fire. It was going to be an inside day. He went into the kitchen, poured a mug of coffee, and sat down in a kitchen chair with the Sunday edition of the *Chicago Tribune*, a luxury that he and Judy enjoyed when they were in New Hampshire.

No sooner had Mark gotten comfortable than he heard a knock on the door. It was Dave Kraft. Donna was writing a sermon, so Dave came in, poured a cup of coffee and sat opposite Mark at the kitchen table.

"How's the Trail, Dave?" Mark asked, anxious to hear another story about Dave's work. He wasn't disappointed. After hearing the latest harrowing accounts of man and beast, he told Dave about his anniversary present to Judy. "Judy tells me that you and Donna took an Alaskan cruise."

"We did," Dave answered. "It was great. It's the only cruise we've ever taken, but we will do it again someday. The scenery was tremendous, especially on the inland part of the trip. Only problem we had was an accident on the cruise ship. A crew member who was painting a cabin balcony fell off the ship."

"A man fell overboard? Did he drown?" Mark asked.

"No, fortunately he was rescued. A passenger on the ship saw him fall and alerted the crew. It took about fifteen minutes for them to recover him and he was already suffering from hypothermia. He was quite a celebrity afterwards. In fact, Donna and I had an occasion to speak with him before the cruise ended. Amazingly, he wasn't shaken by the event. It was difficult to understand him because he spoke with a heavy accent. I think he was from the Philippines. He took it all in stride, said that it was no big deal, that every summer they lose a person or two overboard, usually passengers. I asked whether he was afraid to die. He said drowning is probably the best way if you have to go early. Like a dream, he had been told. Once you breathe in the water, everything goes into slow motion and you simply go to sleep."

Mark could always depend on Dave for a good story. "That must have put a damper on your cruise," Mark said.

"Not really," Dave answered. "The crew member was okay. The trip continued as if nothing had happened. It made us all a little more careful when we were on deck."

The weather on Thanksgiving Eve was dreary. Cloudy skies were heavy with moisture and the temperature was in the low forties. It was dark when Judy and Mark arrived at the church. Donna spoke on "The Gift of Life." In it she acknowledged God as the giver of life in three forms: biological, baptismal, and eternal. Quoting scripture, she cited God's promises relating to each form of life, and how we receive these gifts from Him. Judy felt as though Donna was preaching directly to her which, in fact, she was. She noted that life belongs to God, even when the going gets rough. "Our earthly struggle is for a time," she said, "but the perfect life that God promises is forever. Our earthly life is but a grain of sand on the beach of eternity." Then she quoted St. Paul, *"Our citizenship is in heaven. And we eagerly await a Savior from there, the Lord Jesus Christ, who, by the power that enables him to bring everything under his control, will transform our lowly bodies so that they will be like his glorious body."* Concluding the sermon, she spoke a prayer of thanksgiving to God for His precious gifts of life. The service ended with the hymn

"Praise and Thanksgiving" sung to the tune of Cat Stevens' "Morning Has Broken."

Mark and Judy waited with Dave in the Narthex while Donna greeted the worshipers, changed from her garments, and closed the church. They drove together in the Excursion to the chalet where Mark prepared a late dinner. Judy and Donna set the kitchen table while Dave poured beverages. The mood of the evening was light and no mention was made about the sermon or the message intended for Judy. After dinner Mark opened a case of dominoes and they played Mexican Train for several hours.

"I've always been intrigued by the work of rangers, Dave, and you seem so happy in your job. What do you like most?" Mark asked.

"I like it all. Now that the government owns most of the Appalachian Trail, the Forest Service shares responsibility for the safety of the hikers with local law enforcement agencies, and oversees the work of the Trail volunteers. The Trail is maintained almost entirely by Trail clubs from Georgia to Maine, and most do a great job. In New Hampshire the Appalachian Mountain Club, the United States Forest Service, and state park agencies take strict care of the White Mountain areas. Once in a while someone gets lost or injured, but the most common problem is getting sick hikers off of the trail. Food spoils, or they drink unfiltered water and pick up a bacteria, or they run afoul of a rabid animal. These things are rare but they happen, and the hikers need help. Just about everyone carries a mobile phone now, so our response time is cut down considerably, but the Trail is rugged and getting there takes time.

"What about snakes and bears and the like?" Mark asked, grimacing.

"They're overrated," Dave smiled. "Why don't you join me up here? We need more men with your background."

"Don't tempt me," Mark replied. Dave and Donna helped clean up the kitchen and said goodnight.

Early on Saturday morning Mark finished winterizing and closing up the chalet while Judy packed the Excursion. They left at 7:00 A.M. and headed west. In Massachusetts Judy's right arm jerked so violently that she bruised her elbow on the door handle. They bought elbow pads at a Wal-Mart, then cinched them to Judy's arms with Velcro straps.

Somewhere between Massachusetts and Pennsylvania, Judy worked up the courage to share her fantasies about moving to New Hampshire. She was amazed at Mark's response. He was open to the idea. "Why do you want to move?" he asked.

"This may seem selfish, Mark," she began, "but I feel more protected there. Besides, it seems like the right time."

"Explain," Mark said.

"Well, my work is over in Chicago," she began. "I have to find a new doctor, and I like Dr. Ryan in Woodsville. Dave and Donna are our closest friends. We could make a killing on the townhouse, and the chalet is paid for. That would tide us over until you get settled in a new job. And it is more secluded."

"Wow," Mark replied, "you've really given this some thought. Help me on a few things here. Isn't Dr. Ryan a family doctor?"

"Mark, let's face it," Judy said in a matter-of-fact tone, not seeking sympathy, "I'm not going to get better. There is no miracle cure. No doctor has the answer. The best that they can do is to drug me up until I'm not myself. I'm comfortable with Dr. Ryan."

"I have to confess, Judy," Mark said, "I've considered moving to Woodsville, too." Sometimes Judy hated the wide center console in the Excursion. She missed the old bench seats. At the moment she wanted to slide across and kiss Mark on the neck. Instead she touched his cheek.

"I love you, Mark. I don't know what I ever did to deserve you. You make me so happy."

"You aren't going to cry now, are you?" Mark asked. It made him go crazy when Judy cried.

"No, I'm going to smile," she said. "Mark, what will you do about your work at the police department?"

"I don't know, Judy," he answered. "Dave said something about getting retirement credit for my work at RPD if I hired on with the Forest Service."

"Would you like to do what Dave does?"

"I think I would. It would be different, and I'd have to go through training, but it felt good being on the Trail with Dave yesterday."

"Dave's work isn't always that exciting."

"He told me that there are lonely times," Mark replied. "It's no different in police work."

By the time they crossed into Illinois they had listed the things they would need to do to make the move. At the top of the list was employment. Mark would need to have a job. Second on the list was how to dispose of the furniture in the townhouse. They also considered the pros and cons of selling versus renting the townhouse. There was much to be done.

Mark spent Monday plowing through a week of reports at the police department. Jeff had hired a permanent replacement for Sue, whose name was Roberta, but she preferred Bobby. The department was donut-starved, so when Mark came in with his usual dozen from Dunkin' Donuts he got a round of applause. It was good to be back. Nostalgia was already settling in as Mark considered the future.

Judy poured a cup of coffee into a sipping mug and toasted a bagel. The increasing agitation of her muscles burned more calories than before, and she knew she had to eat more to slow down her weight loss. This was complicated by the chore of eating. She had stabbed her face so often with forks that she ate everything on a spoon, and hot drinks had to be taken in a sipping mug. She decided to read the papers in order by date starting with the previous Monday. A prominent article in Tuesday's local news section caught her attention. She could hardly believe what she was reading. The headlines read, "Explosion at Bio-Gen Laboratories Kills Two." The article continued:

> "An early morning explosion at Bio-Gen Laboratories on the north side of Chicago killed two scientists, Drs. George Palmer and Michele Phillips, and destroyed a research laboratory at the facility. The fire resulting from the explosion was contained in the laboratory by the sprinkler system and the fast response of the Chicago Fire Department. The cause of the fire is being investigated, but it is thought that fumes accumulated under a hood from a Bunsen burner that had not been properly extinguished. Both scientists were working in the laboratory at the time.

The nature of their work has not been disclosed by Bio-Gen management, and the company has made no public statement."

Judy reread the article a second time. She was shocked. George Palmer had been Bob Archer's supervisor. She didn't know Dr. Phillips, but assumed she must have been hired after Bob died. Bob's associate, Dr. Bev Hudson, had spoken often of George, especially after Bob's death, but always spoke well of him. It was an awful tragedy, Judy thought.

The phone interrupted her thoughts. It was Becky Mallott. "Hi, Judy, I wondered if you would like company. We have a teacher's day off and I'm dying to hear about your trip."

Judy was hoping for some time to herself, but invited Becky over. "Come on over, Becky. I've got news."

Kelly barked before the doorbell rang. Becky followed Judy as she walked to the kitchen and saw that Judy's swagger had gotten worse. In the hallway leading from the door to the kitchen, Judy had swayed so far to one side that she brushed the wall, but Becky said nothing. When they got into the kitchen, she poured herself a cup of coffee and sat at the table with Judy. "Bagel?" Judy asked.

"No, thanks. I've eaten," Becky replied. "What's the news?"

"It's not all good," Judy answered. "I just read about the explosion at Bio-Gen."

"It's been on television," Becky said. "Did you know the two who died?"

"George Palmer was Bob's supervisor," Judy answered. "I didn't know the other person."

"I'm sorry, Judy," Becky said, placing her hand on Judy's.

"I didn't know him well," Judy said, "but I do have some good news. Well, I hope you'll receive it as good news." Becky was afraid that Judy was going to tell her that she was pregnant, and she didn't know how she would react. "Mark and I are thinking about moving. You can't say a word to anyone until Mark tells his captain, promise?"

"Of course. Where are you going?" Becky asked.

"Woodsville, New Hampshire!" Judy exclaimed.

Becky was surprised. "Why?" she asked. Judy recited her list of reasons.

"What will you do with the townhouse?"

"We haven't decided. Sell or rent, I suppose," Judy answered.

After a moment Becky said, "You know that Hannah and Marie and I have been trying to find a place that we can rent together. Would you consider renting to three teachers if the price is right?" Hannah and Marie were former colleagues of Judy's that taught at the same high school. She knew them as serious, hard working teachers. Like Becky, they were mature and single. Judy was excited at the prospect.

"It sounds good, but I'll have to discuss it with Mark. Rent around here isn't cheap, but with three splitting the cost it might be manageable. How soon do you need to know?"

"We're all in apartments with leases. We'll have to give some notice. You talk to Mark. I'll talk to the others, okay?" Becky asked, and Judy agreed. Things were beginning to work out.

Bobby knocked tentatively on the door to Mark's office. He beckoned her in. "Good morning, Lieutenant Garrison," she said softly.

"Good morning, Bobby," Mark said. "What's up?"

"You received an email this morning from a Mr. Kraft," she said as she handed a printed copy of the email to Mark, then turned and left the office.

"Thank you," Mark said to the girl's back. She is not Sue, he thought. He read the email.

> Hi, Mark.
> Please call me this evening. I have the information you requested.
> Later, Dave Kraft

There was much to discuss at dinner. Judy began with the news account of the explosion at Bio-Gen. Mark was shocked. Immediately, he thought like a policeman. He knew at once who George Palmer was, and it seemed to Mark too coincidental that another person connected with Bio-Gen had died. So far, the death tally was four—Archer, Hudson, now Palmer and someone named Phillips. He searched his mind for a link. At first, he didn't make a connection between the Bio-Gen deaths and Sue McGrath's death, but this news from Bio-Gen started a low intensity rumble in his subconscious that would not recede.

Then Judy shared her discussion with Becky Mallott. "I know all of these teachers," Judy said, "and I think that they would make good tenants. I'd like to rent to them."

Mark had always considered the townhouse hers, so he quickly agreed. "It will be difficult to manage the townhouse from New Hampshire, Judy. We'll need to have a realtor or property manager watch over things."

"I'll make some calls," she offered. "If I come up with a figure that covers our costs and the costs of management, and if I can download a boilerplate lease from the Internet, should I contact Becky with an offer?"

"Let's agree on the rental cost first," Mark suggested. Judy nodded. Mark excused himself from the kitchen table, then went into the living room to call Dave Kraft. After awhile, Judy joined him in the living room.

"What did Dave say, Mark?" she asked. "And how is Donna?"

"Everyone's great," Mark answered. Referring to his scribbled notes, he summarized Dave's information. "As Dave told me in Woodsville, there are openings in the Forest Service in New Hampshire, but getting into the Forest Service is a little more complicated than I thought, and my age may go against me. I'm older than the cutoff for a permanent Ranger."

"What is a permanent Ranger?" Judy asked.

"There are permanent and seasonal Rangers," Mark answered. "Seasonal Rangers aren't stable. They are moved from area to area as the seasons dictate. Permanent Rangers may remain longer in one location. Dave did say that because the Forest Service is understaffed they are making some hiring exceptions. He feels that my experience will help, and the fact that I am only a few years older than the cutoff may not go against me. I have to tell you, though, I will take quite a cut in pay."

"Can we get by?" Judy asked.

"I think so," Mark answered. "I would have to take an eighteen-week training course at the Federal Law Enforcement Training Center in Glencoe, Georgia."

"What exactly do Rangers do?" Judy asked.

"Law enforcement mainly. They are the forest police. When things are quiet, they have other duties as well, but they are primarily the cops of the wild."

"Is this something that you want to do, Mark?" Judy asked.

"As opposed to the work I'm doing, yes," he answered.

"Are you going to apply to the Forest Service?" she asked.

"Yes," Mark answered.

"Then, it's a done deal," Judy said. "We have tenants for the house, and a new job opportunity in New Hampshire. We're on the way! I'm excited."

"We'll set New Year's Day as the target date for our move," Mark said.

12

Presiding over the monthly Executive Committee meeting, Aaron Krimer asked the others, "Have each of you read the report of the Arson Investigator?" All heads nodded. He withdrew the report from a manila folder on the table in front of him and read the conclusion, which was highlighted in yellow:

> "It is the determination of this investigator that the fire which destroyed the laboratory and office designated as 311 at the Bio-Gen building was caused by the carelessness of an employee while working in the laboratory. The location of the two people killed in this event suggest that Dr. Michele Phillips was closest to the source of the explosion, and that Dr. George Palmer was entering the laboratory at the time of the explosion. Our findings suggest that the explosion occurred when a Bunsen burner was ignited beneath a hood. It is likely that the gas valve had been left partly open allowing a buildup of fumes beneath the hood, and that when an attempt was made to ignite the burner the fumes exploded. The location of Dr. Phillips suggests that she ignited the burner and was killed by the intense explosion. It is possible that Dr. Palmer entered the laboratory on the occasion of the explosion and was overcome by a fire blast when he opened the door leading into the laboratory."

"Gentlemen," Krimer continued, "we must do everything necessary to avoid a civil suit in this matter. Is this clear?" Sanders and Lawson nodded.

"Has there been an assessment of the projects under study when the accident occurred?" A brief pause, almost imperceptible, before the word 'accident' caused Lawson to stir in his chair. Since the explosion he had been uncomfortable with what seemed like a deliberate attempt to avoid discussing the victims or their families.

"Yes," Sanders answered, "the two projects under study in lab 311 were backed up in the computer and can be reestablished very quickly."

"Was any work being done on 15105 there?" Krimer asked.

"No sir," Sanders assured, "15105 is out of product research and in product development." The CEO nodded, but Lawson stared in thought. If 15105 was in product development, what were Palmer and Phillips doing in Lab 311? They were heading up 15105. He pondered. There could have been any number of reasons for them to be in a product research lab; nevertheless, he would stop by the secretary's office in product development and ask to see their sign-out slips for the day of the accident.

Leaving the conference room, Lawson stopped the elevator one floor short of his office area, departed and walked to the reception desk of the product development suite. "Good morning, Sharon," he said to the receptionist with a friendly smile.

"Good morning, sir," she replied. "Is there someone you'd like to see?"

"No, not really, Sharon, but I would like to look at your sign-out ledger." The receptionists of each department were the first lines of defense for company security. Each kept a ledger of who came and went through the main department doors.

"The ledgers are turned into the security department at the end of each month, sir," Sharon replied. "Did you have a particular date in mind?"

"Yes, actually I do," Lawson replied, "the date of the explosion in product research." Sharon referred the CFO again to the security department. He departed and returned to the elevators. The security department was located on the ground floor, immediately behind the main reception desk. The department clerk had no difficulty locating the ledger in question.

"I believe this is what you are looking for," he said as he slid the ledger book across his desk, opened to the day of the explosion. Lawson ran his hand along the entries until he found the name M. Phillips. Next to the name, in the column headed "destination" Dr. Phillips had entered "Lab 311." In the "time out" column she had written "5:25p". It was the "purpose" column that caught the CFO's attention. It read "conference." George Palmer's entry was similar to Dr. Phillips', but there was no entry in the "purpose" column.

Lawson closed the ledger, thanked the clerk, and then walked slowly to the elevators. Why would they have a conference in product research, he wondered. And why at 5:30 P.M. when the Bio-Gen building was usually empty. And why would a conference be held in a lab instead of a conference room, of which there were several in product development. He was still unsettled over the absence of Krimer and Sanders at the Phillips and Palmer funerals. It had always been company tradition for the executives of the company to attend the funerals of company employees, but he was the only one of the group present.

The ding of the elevator on the floor of the finance department snapped his mind back to the matters of the day, but the issue of Phillips and Palmer would not go away. One question kept nagging him—who called the conference?

In mid-December Mark received a letter from the United States Forest Service. To his amazement, he was accepted as a candidate for a Type I position and was scheduled to begin his academy training on January 7. The six-week law enforcement phase of the eighteen-week program would be reduced to two weeks because of his years of experience in law enforcement. He would be required to attend the classroom sessions only. Academy training would conclude on April 12, and he would be assigned to the Hanover office in New Hampshire as requested. Mark wondered how much pressure Dave Kraft had exerted on the Service on his behalf. He dropped the other mail on the floor of the living room and double-stepped upstairs to share the good news with Judy.

Judy was folding clean clothes on the bed when Mark burst into the room. "I got it!" he said, and shoved the letter into her hand. "Everything I asked for, and more!" Judy read the letterhead and quickly skimmed the letter.

"Are you sure this is what you want, Mark?"

"Yes, I am," he answered, sitting next to her on the bed.

"Then we have to move quickly," she said, "if we are going to be settled into the chalet on schedule. What will I do without you for fourteen weeks, and what about our cruise?"

"We'll work those things out, Judy," he said.

Christmas was celebrated at the Garrison townhouse amidst boxes and suitcases. No decorations were put out and no stockings were hung over the fireplace with care. In his hands Mark carried a box wrapped in Christmas colors and tied with a red ribbon and bow. A card bearing Judy's name was tucked into the ribbon. He handed the box to Judy. "This is a special Christmas, Judy. It's our last Christmas in Illinois and in our townhouse." He immediately regretted what he had said. It couldn't escape Judy's mind that any Christmas might be her last. He amended his poor choice of words by adding, "In a few days we will begin a new life and a new job in New Hampshire." They sat down in the living room and Mark asked Judy to open her gift.

"Wait here," Judy said. Slowly she rose from her chair, swayed a bit, then recovering her balance went to the closet in the foyer. She called Mark to the foyer and asked him to remove a cardboard box from the hat shelf in the closet. They returned to the living room. "Your gift came yesterday and I haven't wrapped it. Do you want to open it as it is?"

"Of course," he said. Mark had always considered gift wrapping a waste of good paper. "Who first?" he asked. Judy insisted that Mark go first, knowing that at Christmas he was just a little boy grown tall. He cut the tape, opened the box, and withdrew a Jansport Equinox 33 Daypack— the Cadillac of daypacks. He tore into the daypack, opened Velcro-strapped compartments, adjusted waist and shoulder straps, then slipped the daypack onto his back and strutted up and down the hallway. "This is great! How did you know I would need this?"

"A little elf named Dave told me," Judy said, delighted with Mark's joy. Returning to earth, Mark slipped the daypack from his back, set it on the floor, and gave Judy a bear hug.

"Thanks," he said, then lifted her chin and gave her a lingering kiss, "Now, it's your turn."

With greater appreciation for the wrappings, she untied the bow, released the tape from the paper, and carefully removed the box. Inside, she pulled back the tissue paper and withdrew a brightly-colored short sleeved blouse with a Hawaiian-type print and a pair of blue shorts with pockets. She held the clothes to her and looked at Mark.

"It's winter," she said, smiling, knowing what Mark intended.

"Not in the Caribbean in May," Mark responded. "These are cruise clothes."

Judy laughed, responded with a kiss, and handed Mark his glass of wine. Raising hers, she offered a toast. "Here's to our new life!"

Two days after Christmas all seventeen members of the Riverside Police Department, with the exception of Bobby who was left behind to cover the phones, gathered at Romano's Restaurant for a farewell lunch for Mark. Mark was feted with a roast from his fellow workers and a pair of expensive Scarpa hiking boots made in Italy. In addition, he received a few gag gifts, including a water pistol thought to be all the armament needed in the Forest Service. Mark fought back tears as each member of the force hugged him at the front door of Romano's leaving him with the most important gift of all—memories of his years at the RPD.

Judy, too, received a surprise on the following day. Becky Mallott, Hannah, and Marie, the teachers that were about to move into the townhouse, came surreptitiously to sign the lease, which they did. Afterwards, however, they "kidnapped" Judy and took her to the high school. The four walked through open doors at the main entrance, turned right and walked past the administrative offices, then entered the cafeteria. The school was dark and quiet. As soon as the cafeteria doors opened, the lights came on and a shout of "surprise" was heard up and down the hallways.

Judy was not only surprised, she was stunned. She reeled, and Becky immediately pulled a chair from under a cafeteria table and pushed it under Judy. Thirteen teachers and a cafeteria volunteer gathered around Judy's table and the fun began. Several hours later, with paper plates, cups, and napkins askew on the tables, and wild tales of Judy's career at the high school exhausted, Becky called the group to attention. "Judy, " she said, facing the guest of honor, "we have something that we would like to present to you." She beckoned to Hannah who brought what appeared to be a photo album in a cloth cover with the name "Judy" embroidered on the cover. Becky took the book from Hannah and said, "Your accomplishments in the Literature Department of Riverside High School are not written in your evaluation forms. They are written in every poem, novel, or piece of literature that has or will come from the pens of your students. You have instilled a love for literature here by your own enthusiasm and hard work. In this book are some of the published works of your students, and each one is signed by the writer with a personal wish for you." Becky handed the thick album to Judy who sat speechless for what seemed like an eternity, spilling tears over the album and table.

Gathering her composure, Judy could only say in a broken voice, "I will miss you all." Becky assisted Judy to her feet, and one by one the teachers said goodbye with hugs and final anecdotes. The cafeteria volunteer was last in line. She had packed the remaining pieces of the cake now bearing the letters 'D-Y' in the original baker's box and handed it to Becky.

"Goodbye, Mrs. Garrison," she said, standing at a respectful distance. Judy reached out and hugged her while thanking her for helping with the event. Becky, Hannah, and Marie assisted the volunteer with cleaning the cafeteria, then took Judy home.

There was one final goodbye for Judy, a trip to the cemetery to say goodbye to Bob Archer. With the rented trailer packed and Kelly resting quietly in his travel kennel in the back of the Excursion, Mark parked on the road at Rest Haven Cemetery near the mausoleum where Bob's ashes were interred. He remained in the vehicle while Judy walked to the mausoleum. He watched as she sat on a bench facing the vault bearing Bob's name. Judy placed a rose from one of the centerpieces at her high school luncheon in a container affixed to the opening of the vault.

As Judy allowed her thoughts to form she was struck by the irony of her situation. She was dying of an incurable disease, and Bob had taken his life in the midst of a discovery that had cured others. Unlike Mark, Bob had known of the possibility that Judy could get Huntington's disease when he married her. Was it possible, she thought, that he had risked everything to find a cure for her? "Goodbye, my dear Bob," she said to the vault in front of her. "Rest in eternal peace. I will always love you." She placed her hand on the vault, then turned and walked unsteadily to the car. Mark held her door open, then helped her step into the vehicle. They swung out of the parking lot and turned toward the Interstate. Judy didn't ask Mark why he had not driven past the house in which he grew up. Little was said by either until they had negotiated the expressways out of Chicago and crossed the Indiana border.

Mark stayed alert until they pulled into the gravel area in front of the chalet. Judy had slept for seven hours. Someone had shoveled the snow, clearing a narrow path to the front door. Across the double window to the right of the door hung a banner with carefully painted letters reading, "Welcome home, Mark and Judy." Mark sat quietly looking across Judy's sleeping body at the greeting. This is home, indeed, he thought. What would the future hold for us in this place? He felt blessed as he looked at his beautiful wife resting peacefully and then at the welcome banner, a gift of love from their best friends. Quietly, he prayed a prayer of thanks for the people in his life and for a safe journey. Then he prayed for Judy. After his amen he touched her cheek gently and said, "We're home, honey, and you need to see what the Kraft's have done."

The next morning, just before leaving for Manchester, Mark called United Airlines to check Lois's flight. Judy's mother was going to stay with Judy while Mark was in training. He picked up some fresh fruit from the kitchen and CD's from the living room, patted Kelly on the head, then quietly left the chalet for Manchester.

Mark sat in the main waiting area of the airport, which was small by O'Hare standards, so it wasn't long until he saw Lois waving and walking in his direction. "How was the flight?" he asked as she approached.

"Cramped. What time will you leave tomorrow, Mark?" Lois asked.

"Early. I have to report in at Glencoe on the seventh. Training actually begins on the eighth." The return trip went quickly. Mark briefed Lois on the support that she could expect in Woodsville. Lois took notes, recording the names of Dr. Ryan, Morgan's Drugstore, and Harry Minnick, the retired gentleman who had taken care of the chalet when it was rented. They discussed Judy's condition and the couple's future plans.

Judy was waiting in the guest bedroom sitting by the window that faced the front of the chalet. She saw them arrive and went to the front door. Lois came up the pathway empty-handed, and seeing Judy quickened her pace. They got settled into the chalet while Mark unloaded Lois' things. Donna had prepared lunch before returning to the parsonage, so as soon as Mark finished loading the luggage into the living room the three sat down to eat. Watching Judy eat was an awakening experience for Lois.

Judy awoke with Mark at 5:00 on the following morning. She made a pot of coffee and, with effort, filled Mark's stainless steel thermos and mug. While Lois slept, Mark and Judy clung to each other in the doorway of the chalet. Mark folded back Judy's robe, caressed her breasts, then pulled her naked body close to him. "Get out of here, Mark Garrison," Judy said as she gently pushed him out the door, then closed her robe around her.

"I love you, Judy Garrison," Mark said over his shoulder. Judy stood at the door and watched the Excursion pull away in the dark. She had no way of knowing what the next fourteen weeks would bring.

13

Mark was exhausted when he pulled through the security gates of the federal training center. At the administration building, he received his information packet and bunk assignment. There were six bunks in his room, and each assigned area contained a worktable, chair, and hanging locker. This would be home for the next fourteen weeks.

I'm so glad he can't see me now, Judy thought after Mark had been gone for five weeks. The bruise on her head was turning yellow and would soon be gone. Two weeks earlier she had fallen down the short stairway leading to the bedrooms. Harry Minnick installed a railing on each side of the steps to prevent a recurrence.

Lois was getting used to Judy's condition. After Mark's departure, Lois had time to observe her daughter and was surprised at how fast the symptoms were progressing. It could only mean that the disease had started much earlier than realized. Dr. Ryan was very helpful, having researched Huntington's and gotten a number of helpful brochures for Judy. She was satisfied that Lois could provide medical supervision but did not rule out the eventual need for care in a nursing home. At Judy's regular visit, Dr. Ryan examined her, wrote several prescriptions, then sent the women home.

Because of several choking scares, Lois now cut Judy's solid food into small pieces and pureed vegetables. One of the brochures on eating suggested reducing dairy products because of their tendency to increase mucus, inducing choking. Judy would have no part of it. She was a milk addict and intended to remain so. About this she was adamant, and Lois deferred. Much of their days were spent preparing and eating meals. In addition to cutting and pureeing food, Lois had found special tableware on a Huntington's Website including cups with lids much like travel mugs and plates with suction cups on the bottom. Judy was already resigned to eating with a spoon. Instead of dwelling on the special precautions, Lois made every meal fun by varying the menus and preparing things that Judy liked. Grocery lists, shopping, and cooking became games for the women, and Judy was never outwardly morose about her special needs or advancing symptoms. Inwardly, however, it was a different matter.

Two days after Valentine's Day, Kelly died. He failed to return from a backyard toilet excursion. Harry Minnick found his body in the crawl space under the chalet. When the truth took hold, Judy broke into sobs and laid her head on her arms. Both Lois and Harry Minnick stood silently as their own tears flowed.

At 7:00 the next morning, Dave, Donna, Lois, Judy, and Harry Minnick gathered around the grave that Harry had dug behind the shed. Donna said a prayer beseeching God to show mercy on all his creatures, and especially this day on Kelly. Lois supported Judy as she lifted Kelly into his final resting-place. They all watched as Harry covered the grave, then placed a makeshift cross on the mound, which would be replaced in time by a proper marker.

After everyone had left, Judy returned to the grave while Lois watched from the kitchen.

Her fear of black snakes notwithstanding, she lay down on her side next to the gravesite and rested her head near the cross. Out loud she thanked God for Kelly and for his peaceful death in old age, wondering whether it was proper to ask for the same favor for her. A light snow had fallen during the morning, so Lois offered to help Judy inside before she caught cold. Two days went by before she was able to email the news to Mark, and even then she shed tears on her keyboard.

In the evening Judy sat with her mother in the kitchen. "Did Daddy ever talk about me?" she asked, looking into her mother's face.

"Oh, Judy, of course he did," Lois answered. "He loved you very much. It was his idea that you not see him after he was bedridden. Whenever he heard you going by his room or heard the music from your radio upstairs he would grow calm and attentive."

"Why didn't you tell me what was going on, Mom?"

"I didn't think that you would be able to handle it. Perhaps it was a mistake."

"Weren't you afraid that I would get the disease?"

"I was terrified until Bob ..." Her mother stopped suddenly.

"Bob what?" Judy asked, shifting in her position and withdrawing from her mother's hand to face her.

"Nothing," Lois said. "We've talked enough."

"Bob what?" Judy said insistently.

"I'm sorry, Judy, but I've known for a long time that you had Huntington's, and I tried to get you to be tested so that you could find out for yourself, but you refused."

"How did you know?" Judy asked. "Tell me at once."

"Bob did a DNA test," Lois said.

"I never submitted to that," Judy said, puzzled.

"He used a hair, Judy," Lois said. Judy stumbled to her feet and staggered into the kitchen. Lois followed.

"Do you mean that you have known all along that I have Huntington's and never told me?" Judy said angrily.

"You refused to be tested, Judy," Lois asserted. "We thought it would be better for you to know at your own time. What would you have done?"

"And Bob knew? Is this why he didn't want a family?" Judy asked of no one in particular. "Is this why he became obsessed with his project? Is this why he took his life? Oh, my God!" Judy said, burying her head in her hands and sobbing. Lois came into the kitchen and stood behind Judy, holding her heaving shoulders. As suddenly as she began sobbing she stopped. She rose from the table and slowly walked to the steps leading up to the bedroom hallway. At the steps she turned to Lois. "Did Dad know?"

"No, I didn't tell him. You know how much he loves you, Judy."

"How about Mark?" Judy asked, not sure that she wanted to hear the answer.

"No," Lois answered. "I was the only one besides Bob who knew."

"I can't believe that you did this," Judy said. "It is my life. I had a right to know."

"Bob told me that he had made a discovery in his laboratory," Lois said. "He was very excited. He knew your history and your risk and thought that his discovery might be useful if you developed Huntington's."

"I know about his work, Mom," Judy said, "but he never told me that he was doing it for me. When did he learn that I had Huntington's?"

"When his work looked promising, he submitted a hair sample for DNA testing, then found the Huntington gene. He wanted so badly to have a cure for the disease before telling you, Judy," Lois said.

"Then why did he …" Judy started to ask.

"Kill himself?" Lois finished. "I don't know. Perhaps something went wrong. Perhaps he couldn't handle the thought of losing you." Without another word Judy went slowly up the steps to her room.

The next morning Judy asked her mother to take her to the parsonage. "I'm going to see Donna today," she said. Lois helped Judy get dressed and drove her to the parsonage. She sat in the Escort and watched until Judy was at the door of the parsonage. Donna opened the door and Judy stepped inside.

Donna could not recall seeing the grimace. She had seen Judy angry on occasion, but her anger didn't last. Now, Judy looked as though her anger was etched on her face. Her eyes were narrow, her eyebrows pursed together, and her lips drawn to a slit. She tried to greet Judy with a hug, but Judy stood stiffly with her arms hanging straight at her sides. There were no tears, just a grimace. Donna wasn't familiar enough with Huntington's to know that this was a symptom. Lois had seen the grimace and knew that over time this would become constant. "Come in, Judy," Donna said, releasing her hands from Judy's shoulders. "Judy, I can tell that something is wrong. Would you like to discuss it?"

"My mother and Bob have known all along that I have Huntington's and never told me," Judy blurted. Donna sat silently waiting for more, but nothing more came.

"Did your mother tell you why she kept this a secret?" Donna asked.

"She didn't think that I could handle it."

"Is she right?"

"I don't know," Judy conceded, "but I feel deceived."

"Sometimes, silence is the better course," Donna suggested.

"Who makes that decision?" Judy asked.

"Paul wrote to the Ephesians that part of maturing in our faith is speaking the truth in love. What do you think that means, Judy?" Donna asked. Judy shrugged. "To me it means that there are some things that are better left unsaid in the interest of love. If I didn't like the dress you're wearing, what would be gained by my saying so? Perhaps Bob and your mother felt that telling you would cause more harm than good. After all, Judy, you refused to be tested. It was apparent that you didn't really want to know. Isn't that true?" Judy shrugged again. "Do you think," Donna continued, "that they wanted to hurt you?"

"No," Judy conceded after a few seconds.

"Do you think that it was easy for them, knowing that you had Huntington's and letting you discover it on your own? I'm sure that there were times when they wanted to tell you, but bore the secret to let you live your life a while longer before having to deal with the truth."

Judy lowered her head into her hands and cried. After a moment she said, "Please call my mother and have her pick me up."

"I'll take you home, Judy," Donna offered.

The Escort was gone when Donna pulled into the parking area so she walked with Judy into the chalet. Within minutes Lois came through the front door with an armload of groceries. She set the bag down on the kitchen counter, removed a quart container of Ben and Jerry's ice cream, then put two scoops in each of two dishes.

"Guess what this is?" she asked.

"Okay, Mom, what is it?"

"Chunky Monkey," Lois answered as she put the bowls on the table. "Today you are going to have dairy." Alternately she fed herself and Judy until the treat was finished.

"I had almost forgotten," Judy said. Chunky Monkey was reserved for those times when a person needed cheering up. "Thanks, Mom."

"Are we friends?" Lois asked.

"I love you, Mom," Judy answered and placed her hand on her mother's cheek.

Unable to squelch the nagging suspicion that the deaths of doctors Palmer and Phillips were neither accident nor carelessness, Keith Lawson returned to the security department office and asked to speak to the Chief of Security. "How can I help you, Mr. Lawson," the Chief said as the CFO appeared in his doorway.

"May I have a few minutes?" Lawson asked.

"Come in, please. Have a seat," the Chief said as he moved several manila folders from the only visitor's chair in his cluttered office. Lawson closed the door behind him and sat down.

"I'm not as well versed on security matters as I probably should be," he confessed, "and I'd like to ask a question about procedures." He waited for an acknowledgement, but got none. "Do you record internal phone conversations?" he continued.

"The answer is yes. We started doing it when an audit indicated that there were a large number of personal long distance calls being made on company phones. When we announced that calls would be randomly monitored, the abuse stopped."

"What happens to those tapes?" Lawson asked.

"Nothing, really. We can only listen to them with the permission of the caller or a court order, so they are stored for awhile, then reused. Actually, I don't think we've ever listened to any of them. It's like putting a fake alarm sticker on your car window. The threat of listening gets the job done."

"One more question. Is it possible to know from the tapes who called who and when?"

"No, it isn't. It's only possible to know which instrument called which instrument and when," the Chief answered.

"And the tapes are stored so that a particular call can be identified?" Lawson persisted.

"If it occurred within the last six months or so. That's about how long we keep the tapes before they're reused," the Chief answered. "Do you have a particular tape you're interested in, sir?" the Chief asked, hoping to move the conversation along.

"Perhaps," Lawson answered, "but if I understand you correctly I'll need a court order."

"Technically, yes, but if you give me an idea of what you're looking for, I might be able to help." the chief said. Lawson asked the chief to make a written record of all calls made to Dr. Palmer or Dr. Phillip's offices during the week preceding the lab explosion.

"I'd like to keep this between us for now, Chief," Lawson asked. "And call me when you have the information, please, but do not listen to the tapes. Just record the calling stations and the dates, okay?" The chief agreed.

Lawson returned to his office and called Louise Gordon. "Well, for goodness sake," Louise Gordon said, "how are you, Mr. Lawson? It's been a long time."

"Keith, please," Lawson suggested. "How are you?"

"Getting along, Keith. How is Frederick?"

"At U. of I., Louise, can you believe it?"

"I knew he'd make something of himself. Always had that feeling. Congratulations!"

Louise Gordon was Captain of the Chicago Police Department precinct in which the Lawson family lived. At age fourteen, Frederick Lawson, Keith's only son, got in trouble with the police. The matter was soon resolved. During the episode Keith Lawson learned that Louise Gordon shared his enthusiasm for amateur photography. They became friends.

"It's been too long, Louise. How about lunch?" Keith asked. They scheduled lunch for the following day.

Keith Lawson was already seated at a booth in the storefront Chinese restaurant when Louise Gordon entered. "Hi," she said, extending her hand.

"Hi back," Keith replied. The two went through the buffet line and returned to the booth with their assortment of Chinese dishes and won ton soup. "It's good to see you. It's been too long."

"Actually, Keith, I haven't done a lot with my camera lately. Now that spring is here and the colors are out I'll be taking a few photo hikes. How about you?"

"Same, although I did get some great shots on a cross-country ski trip in Wisconsin," Keith said. They continued to talk photography while they ate, and then Keith got to the real reason for arranging their meeting. "I have to confess, Louise, that I have another reason for wanting to see you today." She raised her eyebrows and leaned back against the booth waiting for Keith to continue.

Louise Gordon was a divorcee with two children and the first woman to be promoted to the rank of Captain in the Chicago Police Department. She and Mark Garrison had become friends during the investigation of the events following Bob Archer's death. Because of the investigation, she was somewhat familiar with Bio-Gen.

Keith Lawson trusted her. "Louise, I'm going to share something with you that has nothing to do with photography. I'm not sure it is anything more than my own overactive imagination, but I need for you to hear this."

"You've got my interest up, Keith. Is this police business or personal?"

"Probably police business, if it is anything," Keith said. Louise knew Keith as a sensible and thoughtful man not likely to get carried away.

"Fire away. I'm not in a particular hurry."

"Two scientists at Bio-Gen died in what the CFD Arson Investigator claimed was an act of carelessness. Are you familiar with the case?"

"Yes. In a lab, I believe," Gordon replied. "But you don't think it was carelessness?"

"You're ahead of me, Louise, and you're right. I'm not a policeman or an investigator, but my instincts tell me that there was more involved than carelessness or accident."

"And you're asking me to check into it—based on instinct?" she asked.

"I don't know. That's for you to decide. You may think that I'm overreacting." Lawson told Louise about the absence of Krimer and Sanders at the Palmer and Phillips funerals, and their reluctance to discuss the event of their deaths.

"That's not much to go on, Keith," she said.

"There's more," he continued. "First, those two scientists were assigned to another department and had no business being in the lab where they died. Second, the so-called accident occurred after closing hours. Third, they were two outstanding scientists who would not have left a Bunsen burner valve open, especially under a collecting hood."

"Why were they there?" Louise asked, her curiosity growing.

"That's what I wanted to know so I did some checking," Keith answered. "I checked the sign out sheets in their regular departments. Both signed out to Lab 311 where the accident occurred. Michele Phillips noted that she was going to attend a conference. George Palmer didn't indicate his purpose. It seems unlikely that a conference would be held in a lab after hours just doors away from the conference room. I then had security check the phone records for Michele and George for the week before the event. Both received calls from the Chief Executive Officer of Bio-Gen on the day of the event. I can't listen to the calls without his permission or a court order, but I have the calling and receiving stations and the times and dates. I don't want to tip my hand to the CEO at this point, just in case I'm going up a blind alley."

"What are you expecting to hear?" Louise asked.

"I want to know who called the after-hours conference in Lab 311 and why," Keith answered. "It may tell us more than we already know about the cause of the so-called accident."

"Are you suggesting homicide, Keith?"

"This thing won't go away, Louise," Keith answered, avoiding her question. "I can't shed my suspicions."

"There's more to this than you're telling me."

"Yes, there is," he admitted. "George and Michele were aware of a situation at Bio-Gen that could have been disastrous for the future of the company if it had become known."

"Who knows about this besides you, Keith?" Louise asked.

"The Executive Committee."

"Who's on that committee?"

"Rory Sanders, Aaron Krimer, and myself."

"And you feel strongly enough about this to implicate your colleagues?" Louise asked. "You know what this may mean for you."

"That's not important, Louise. If my colleagues had anything to do with the death of these two scientists, I want no part of them or Bio-Gen," Keith said. "But I'm not ready to point the finger at anyone. That's why I need your help."

"What do you want me to do?"

"Listen to the phone tapes," he replied. "If you hear Aaron Krimer invite Michele and George to a conference in Lab 311 on the day of their death, open an investigation."

"The Arson Investigator already closed his investigation. I'll need more than a phone call to commit our department to a full-scale investigation."

"Does that mean you won't help, Louise?" Keith asked.

"No. I'll get back to you after I've listened to the phone tapes," Louise promised.

"Can you keep me out of this, Louise?"

"For now, perhaps, but not forever. You are a part of the Executive Committee. Frankly, Keith, I wish we had stuck to photography," she said as she rose to leave. "Stay tuned," she said extending her hand, then turned and left the restaurant.

14

There was no training scheduled on Sundays. By the end of his eighth week Mark had developed a routine for the day. He would begin by attending worship service at the Protestant chapel and then call home on his mobile phone. Racquetball at the center courts was followed by an early dinner at a Mexican restaurant in Glencoe, then back to the barracks where he would watch TV in the day room, read another chapter in his mother's book, then go to bed.

On March second he was ready for the final chapter of "And the Greatest of These." As he rearranged the pillows on his bunk, he wondered why he had waited so long to read the book. Inside himself he knew the answer. It was for the same reason that he had fled his home after high school and enlisted in the Army. He could no longer put up with the chaos in his home. The 'aholism's in his family had destroyed his respect for his parents and deprived him of any meaningful relationship with them. The Army was the right choice. There was no time for self-pity or bitter feelings. His mind was focused on survival issues at the basest level, and he was able to take inventory of who he was and where he was headed.

He opened his mother's book to the final chapter and was surprised to find a small flattened envelope tucked tightly into the binding bearing the name, "Mark Dearest." The envelope flap was inserted into the envelope rather than sealed. Mark pulled the flap free and removed the contents. The note was written in small cursive letters on both sides of a single sheet of plain stationary. Mark turned the page over and read the closing, "Love, Mother." His heart rate began to quicken, and he felt a thickening in his throat. Soon his eyes were watering and he had to swallow repeatedly to get air into his lungs. He knew what was happening, but he wasn't sure why.

Mark had read all but one chapter of "And the Greatest of These," his mother's first, and as far as Mark knew, her only published novel. It was a story about a family that survived the Great Depression. It was obvious that the fictional family was Mark's family. In the book the mother told the story. It was Mark's mother telling the story of her life, and it melted Mark's heart. For the first time he was able to look into his mother's soul and vicariously share her pain. Feelings formerly frozen had poured out on Mark's pillow for weeks as he read chapter after chapter. The feelings were a blur, a confluence of love, guilt, and pain. He set the book aside and began to read the letter.

> *My Dearest Mark,*
>
> *You are only a boy. In my heart you will always be my boy even though you will soon be a man. In another year you will finish high school and then you will leave our home and find your own way in the world. I know that whatever choices you make in life will be the right ones. I have seen your strength and determination to be your own person.*
>
> *I have also seen you pull away from your father and me, and I want you to know that I understand. We, too, have grown apart. If I had my way, my dearest son, I would start over and do things differently, but that is not the way of life. It is my prayer (yes, I do pray) that you will discover along the way just how deeply your father and I love you and how much confidence we have in you, even if we haven't always shown it.*
>
> *This book is the story of our life as a family. It is not a guide- book for how a family ought to live. It is the story of a family with flaws. You will discover as you form your own family that all families have flaws, some greater than others. If I could impress anything on you, dearest boy, let it be this, that when you find the woman that God has chosen for you, and you will, love her with all of your being, second only to God himself. And let that love overflow to your chil- dren, every day in every way.*
>
> *My dream now is to be a better mother, a good mother-in-law,*

and a great grandmother. I don't know what the future will hold for
me or for you, but always remember that your mother and father love
you.

    Love, Mother

Mark let the tears pour. For the first time in his memory he pulled out all the stops and sobbed until his heaving chest hurt. He wanted his mother alive and there where he could hold her and beg her forgiveness for his failure as a son, but it was too late for that. Instead, he looked toward the ceiling of his room and asked God to forgive him. In that moment all of the self-pity and bitterness he felt toward his parents left him. It would never return.

On Monday morning Mark was summoned to the Administration Building to see the Training Coordinator. He checked the room directory in the reception lobby and walked one flight to the Coordinator's office. The door was partly open. "Hello," Mark said, peering into the office.

"Can I help you?" the Coordinator asked as he rose from his chair and walked toward Mark.

"Yes, I'm Mark Garrison. You wanted to see me?"

"Yes, Mark. Thank you for coming. I need to go over your program with you. Would you like some coffee?"

"No thanks," Mark said.

"Please have a seat," the TC offered. Mark sat and waited for him to begin.

"Mark, there is a slight change in your training schedule. As you know, because of your experience in law enforcement we waived the weapons and encounter segments of your course. In doing so, however, we are now out of sync with the two-week segment on federal law. That would normally have followed weapons and encounter. We have contacted the university system in New Hampshire. They have a rather comprehensive criminal justice program at Plymouth State College that includes a course on federal law enforcement. The course is taught two sessions per week during the summer. This means that we could conclude your training in Glencoe in several weeks and send you back to New Hampshire to begin on-site training with Ranger Kraft. When you successfully complete the course in Plymouth you will be assigned a position on the Appalachian Trail. We will, of course, pay all the expenses incurred at Plymouth. This is the only way that we can coordinate your program. Is this agreeable with you?"

"Very much so," Mark answered.

"Good. Then here is what you should do. Return to your program today. Your present cycle will end on March twenty-first. Your work has been outstanding to date. Assuming that you complete the next several weeks without incident, you will be conditionally advanced to field training effective April seventh with Ranger Kraft. That will give you a week to get home, get enrolled at Plymouth, and get started with Kraft. Any questions?"

"No, sir," Mark answered. He rose, shook hands, then left the office. The minute he left the Administrative Building he called Judy on his mobile phone to share the news. "Guess what?" he said after Lois put Judy on the phone. "I'm going to be home early!"

"Have you been kicked out?" Judy teased.

"Better than that," he said, ignoring her tease. "I'm going to be able to finish my formal training at Plymouth State rather than Glencoe."

"What is Plymouth State?" Judy asked. Mark explained the plans. "When will you be arriving here?"

"On Sunday night, March twenty-third," Mark answered, "if I don't drive through."

Exhausted, Mark arrived in Woodsville as planned on March twenty-third just before dinner. As he came through the door the living room exploded with shouts of "surprise" as the Kraft's, Lois, Judy, and Harry Minnick wearing a chef's apron surrounded him with hugs and handshakes. The party lasted through dinner after which Harry closed up the charcoal cooker, cleaned the kitchen, and said goodbye. Mark regaled the rest with stories from Glencoe, then said goodbye to Dave and Donna.

Lois and Judy went to their bedrooms, and while Lois was helping Judy get ready, Mark walked to the rear of the shed to visit Kelly's grave. After a few moments of silence, he bent down, patted the mound and thanked the dog. He joined Judy in the bedroom and they talked until after midnight. Judy's disease and medications had not diminished her libido, but she wasn't certain that she would be able to control her spasms. Her prayers were answered. Spent, they slept soundly.

Mark unloaded Lois' luggage at the curbside of the Manchester Airport, then waited with Lois while she was checked in and got her boarding pass. He said goodbye at the security-screening booth. "There's no way that I can thank you, Lois, for what you've done."

"Judy is my daughter, Mark. She has always been a source of pride for me and I will always love her, just as I loved her father. Always remember that you can call me at anytime of the day or night."

They hugged for a long time, then Mark released Lois and she proceeded to her gate.

Excited about his weeks of training Mark wanted to share his enthusiasm for his new job with Judy, but Judy wasn't there. Unlike the night of his return, she had receded into herself. "I want to die," were the first words that he heard her say. She was seated in the recliner in the living room when he returned home, wearing sweatpants and a sweatshirt that covered her knee and elbow pads. She had her knees pulled up and her arms wrapped around them as if to hold everything in place.

Mark poured juice into a covered mug. He placed the mug next to her on a table and it sat there until he retrieved it on Thursday morning. It wasn't until then that Mark discovered the suction-cup plates and was told in no uncertain terms by Judy that he needed to wrap her robe belt around the chair while she ate.

It took time for Judy to fall asleep, but when she did she was perfectly at peace. Not so with Mark. He sat in front of the late spring fire until past midnight gazing at the dying embers and praying for his wife. Quietly, he slipped into their bedroom and slid between the sheets. Instinctively, Judy turned his direction and raised her head onto his shoulder, laying her arm across his chest. Mark felt her warmth and touched her hair lightly. It had the fresh smell he loved. "Why, Lord, why?" he asked silently in a mixture of resentment and resignation.

• • •

When they woke in each other's arms, Mark said, "You scared me last night."

"I'm sorry. I get so angry, then hate myself for it."

"I'm not talking about that. You said that you wanted to die."

"I do, Mark," she confirmed. "Don't be angry with me. It isn't my first choice. My first choice would be to get well, but that isn't in the cards. You know it and I know it. Mom and I talked a lot about the end of Daddy's life. There is no need for us to go through that. You don't know what is ahead for you, Mark, or for me. Even now, I can't remember things, can't control my emotions, my body is out of control and I'm losing weight no matter how much I try to eat. The only thing that I can do well is sleep, and I'd like not to wake up."

"Remember what Donna told you, Judy?" Mark said. "Life belongs to God."

"Mark, would God want me to live like this?" Mark had no answer. "You will have to help me."

"That is out of the question, Judy. I could never do anything like that." Judy waited before she spoke.

"Would you rather that I flail my way to the grave, Mark, like some lunatic?" Judy asked, raising her voice. Mark pulled her close and placed his hand lightly across her mouth. Judy did not resist him.

"Shh," he said. "Quiet. Let's talk about this and try not to get angry. Of course, I don't want you to do that, Judy."

"Then you'll help me?"

"I can't promise that, Judy. I'm sorry." They lay together silently until Mark said, "We have four days with nothing to do but relax. What would you like to do?" Judy looked at Mark sadly.

The April meeting of the Executive Committee of Bio-Gen had just heard the report of the new Director of Product Development. All were pleased with the progress of the human studies of Project 15105. Studies were set up to begin in four major medical centers located in Los Angeles, Minneapolis, Baltimore, and Houston. Controlled experiments would begin in May. Since the gene repair had broad applications, patient eligibility was the last remaining issue to be resolved. A committee comprised of representatives from each of the medical centers was scheduled to meet with the Medical Director of Bio-Gen in late April to establish criteria for participation in the study.

The Executive Committee meeting was close to completion when the conference room telephone rang. CFO Keith Lawson answered the phone, then handed it to Aaron Krimer as Sanders and Lawson listened. "Hello," the CEO said. After a pause, he said, "Well, we're in the middle of a meeting here. Is this something that can wait?" Another pause, then, "Hold on just a minute, I'm going to put you on the speaker." He cupped his hand over the phone, looked at the Committee, and said, "This is the Chief of Security. There are two people downstairs from the Chicago Police Department with a warrant. Listen to this." He then pushed the speaker button on the telephone and replaced the handset in its cradle. "You're now speaking to the Executive Committee," he said to the Chief of Security. "Tell us again what is going on down there."

"Two people from the Chicago Police Department have a warrant stating that they can remove telephone surveillance tapes for the week preceding the accident in Lab 311. What shall I tell them?" the security chief asked.

"Tell them nothing and give them nothing until I have someone from the legal department down there, do you understand?" Krimer insisted. The security chief understood.

"I'll call you from the security department," the senior attorney from the legal department promised in response to Krimer's urgent phone request. The Executive Committee remained in the conference room. In ten minutes the conference room phone rang again. "The warrant is perfectly legal. I've informed the security chief to turn over the tapes. These people are operatives and can't tell me why the tapes are needed. Do you have any idea?" he asked Krimer.

"None, but I would like to see you in my office in the next ten minutes," Krimer said. He then ended the meeting and promised to keep the others informed.

Understanding Keith Lawson's sensitive position, Captain Gordon called him at his home at 10:00 P.M. to report that the detectives assigned to the Bio-Gen case had received a report from their tech lab confirming calls from Krimer's office to the telephones of doctors Palmer and Phillips. She now needed someone familiar with the voices to listen to the tapes. She asked Lawson to come to her precinct office on the following day. He agreed.

The extended play tapes required special equipment, so Captain Gordon took Keith to the tech lab on the following morning to hear the conversations. A police technician had set up the two conversations between Krimer and each of the scientists. He began with the call to George Palmer's office.

"George, good morning," the CEO said when Dr. Palmer answered his telephone. "How are you?"

"Fine, thank you, and you?" Palmer responded.

"Fine, George. Listen, I have a matter that I'd like to review with you, but it will have to wait until the end of the day. Will you be busy at 5:30 this afternoon?"

"I can shift my schedule. What's the subject?" George asked.

"It's a personal thing, George. My grandson is taking a class in chemistry and has asked me a question that I can't answer. I know that you will be able to help. Can we meet in one of the labs in product research? How about 311? I'm sure that the small experiment won't take more than a few minutes. I'd really appreciate your help."

"All right, I'll be there," George agreed, but there was clear irritation in his voice.

"What do you think, Keith," Louise Gordon asked after hearing the tape.

"No doubt," Keith answered. "It's Krimer and Palmer."

"Play the next tape," Captain Gordon said to the lab technician. The conversation between the CEO of Bio-Gen and Dr. Michele Phillips was essentially the same with one important difference. At the end of the conversation, Krimer asked Dr. Phillips to make certain that the Bunsen burner in Lab 311 was working. He would need heat for his experiment. "Is that Dr. Phillips?" Louise asked.

"That's Krimer and Phillips," Keith Lawson responded. "Now what happens?"

"We have enough information to open an investigation, Keith. There doesn't seem to be any doubt that the scientists were set up for the explosion. I'm going to keep my detectives on the investigation until we can question Mr. Krimer. You keep a low profile for awhile, but eventually I'm going to need your testimony. You understand that, don't you, Keith?"

"Of course. What will the detectives be looking for?"

"We'll need to seal off the lab, search it thoroughly, then try to find more evidence to connect the CEO. Your testimony will be enough to provide motive," Louise replied. "For now, it would be helpful for you to keep your ears open."

"Hello, Mr. Garrison," the receptionist said as Mark entered the office.

"Hi," Mark answered. "Is Dr. Ryan here? I don't have an appointment, but I'd like to talk with her, if possible."

"I'm sorry, sir, but she is just about to leave for a very late lunch," the receptionist answered. As she spoke, Dr. Ryan came into the reception area.

"Hi, Mark," she said. "Is there something wrong?"

"In a way," Mark replied. "I was hoping to talk with you."

"I was just going to grab a late lunch. Want to come along? I'll let you pick up the tab. It'll be cheaper than an office visit. I'm a light eater."

"You're on," Mark said as he followed the doctor through the front door. They walked at a quick pace to a pizza shop where Dr. Ryan ordered a cold-cut grinder.

"It's a bit cool, but I like to eat on the picnic tables in the back yard," Dr. Ryan said, leading Mark through doors labeled "picnic area." Mark followed, carrying a Coke and a small bag of potato chips.

"Now, Mark, tell me what's on your mind."

"Judy has a death wish," he said bluntly, "and she wants me to help."

"Suicide is high among Huntington's patients, so the literature says. You're probably already aware of that," Dr. Ryan said.

"I am, and I can understand why, but I could never bring myself to help Judy die."

"Neither could I, Mark, if that's where this conversation is heading."

"Is assisted suicide legal in New Hampshire, Dr. Ryan?" Mark asked.

"Not yet, but it appears as though we may be headed that way. It gets closer with every legislative session. All the states are watching Oregon. There is a ground swell among medical practitioners there to reverse the ruling. Right now it's unlawful for a doctor to assist a patient in ending his or her life in New Hampshire."

"If it isn't too personal, doctor, can you tell me where you stand on the issue?"

"It's not too personal, Mark. In fact, I've been very outspoken against assisted suicide. For me it's a matter of conflict. I've been trained and have sworn to uphold life. There are times, of course, when there are decisions that must be made at the end of some lives whether to extend the process of dying by extraordinary measures, such as tube feeding, respiratory assistance, or shock resuscitation. When the patient is terminally ill and able to assist with the decision, I will honor his or her choice, even if it means that death will come sooner rather than later. If there is hope of recovery I go for broke. That's my job. Death is always my enemy, except when it is inevitable and there are no treatment options."

"But, doctor, that's the situation with Judy, right?"

"Of course it is, but her death is not imminent as far as we know," Ryan answered. "She may go on for years."

"That's exactly what scares her," Mark rebutted. "The thought of going on for years and getting progressively worse motivates her death wish."

"Mark, I've done my homework on this disease, mainly for you and Judy, and I have an idea of what's ahead for her. Believe me, it's not pretty. I can understand why Judy is afraid, but I will not assist her death wish. When the end is near, I will honor her wishes regarding extraordinary care, but that is all you can expect from me. I hope you understand," the doctor said, rising and placing her paper waste in a trash container. "Now, I must get back to my office. My heart goes out to you both, Mark, and I will gladly refer you to a good counselor who may be able to help you, if you are interested."

"I have an excellent counselor already, but thank you," Mark said.

Judy was sitting in the screened-in porch when Mark returned from his chores and his visit with Dr. Ryan. "What took so long?" Judy asked as he carried groceries into the kitchen. He had no intention of mentioning his visit with Dr. Ryan. He didn't want Judy to know that he had given any consideration to her death wish.

"It took a little longer than I expected," he said, hoping the conversation would end. It did.

"Should we cancel the cruise, Mark?" Judy asked.

"Where did that come from?"

"Think of it, Mark. You in your tux and me in my evening dress all set for the Captain's dinner, then you get out my suction plates, plastic-coated spoon, bib, and proceed to feed me pureed lobster!" Mark tried not to laugh, but the moment his expression changed they both laughed uproariously. Then Judy turned serious. "It is funny, Mark, but you know it's true. Just about the time that you introduce me to someone on the cruise, I may say something really nasty, or have a spasm and knock his or her hat overboard. How would you handle that?" Mark knew that Judy was serious and, in fact, he had wondered about the cruise, too.

"Since we know so little about cruises, it might be helpful to talk to Dave and Donna. They might be able to give us some advice.

"Judy and I want to pick your brains tonight," Mark said as the four sat down in the chalet kitchen

Dave said, "Good luck. I'm afraid that the pickings are going to be slim from my end."

Judy asked the leading question, "Do you think that Mark and I should cancel our plans to go on a cruise?"

Donna jumped in. "Heavens, no! Why would you do that?" she asked.

"You have been helping Mom take care of me for the past twelve weeks," Judy said. "You know how I behave. Would you want to take me on a cruise?"

"I'd take you anywhere and be proud of you," Donna said, reaching across the table and touching Judy's hand. "Besides, on a cruise everyone does their own thing. They have activities for every passenger, including passengers with special needs."

"What about eating arrangements?" Mark asked.

"You choose whether you want to eat in the formal dining room, or in the more casual buffet area, or at the snack bar. You can eat in your cabin if you prefer. There are lots of options," Dave said.

"Will I have trouble getting my footing on the boat?" Judy asked.

"It depends on the sea conditions," Dave said. "Cruise ships have stabilizers that keep them steady in the ocean, but if you run into high seas you may want to do what many of the other passengers will be doing—stay in your cabin until things settle down. Actually, May is a pretty quiet month in the Caribbean."

"I hope that you're not considering canceling your trip," Donna said.

"What do you think, Mark?" Judy asked.

"We've made all the preparations, including our passports," he answered. "It would be a shame to waste it, wouldn't it?" With the decision made, they relaxed and enjoyed their evening. Dave and Donna shared stories from their Alaskan cruise, including the story about the crewmember that fell overboard. Mark was curious about how that could happen.

"It's not difficult, Mark," Dave said. "On the top decks, or on the balconies of the expensive cabins you are restrained by railings that are only waist high. In fact, on the upper deck you can look over the railing directly into the water from a height of six stories, maybe more. The crew member who went overboard was part of a painting crew, but a passenger has to be just as careful."

"What would happen if a passenger fell overboard?" Judy asked. "Would they ever find him or her?"

"It depends," Dave answered, "whether anyone saw the accident. If no one saw it happen, it could be days before that person would be missed, if ever. There is no headcount, you know. It's not like being in prison."

"But surely the person would be missed at the end of the cruise," Judy said.

"I don't know how," Donna said. "They never did collect our boarding cards, did they, Dave?"

"Not that I recall."

"Boarding cards?" Mark asked.

"Yes, when you first come on board you are given a boarding card. It looks like a credit card. All of your extra expenses are charged on that card, and it is scanned every time you get off and on the ship, except at the end. They don't scan the card at the final point of debarkation."

"Why do they scan it at all?" Judy asked.

"To make sure that every one who gets off at the various ports gets back on again, or is accounted for. I can remember several delays leaving ports because some of the people who were scanned off hadn't returned. The crew is not happy when passengers are late returning."

"In other words, if someone didn't disembark at the end of the cruise, they wouldn't be missed, would they?" Mark asked.

"Are you planning to get lost at sea?" Donna asked. They all laughed.

Dave and Mark made plans for the following day—Mark's first on the Trail.

While Mark was gone, Harry had come, but he was too late to prevent the gallon bottle of milk from slipping out of Judy's hands onto the kitchen floor, into which Judy had fallen while trying to prevent the accident. Soaked in milk she had attempted to negotiate a shower and fell again doing no damage except to her patience and pride. Eventually, she got into dry clothes and Harry cleaned up the milk in the kitchen. In an effort to preserve some independence, she then tried to prepare grilled cheese sandwiches for she and Donna, but forgot to butter the bread. The smell of burnt bread permeated the chalet when Donna arrived. It was evident that part-time help was no longer suitable.

Donna could see that Judy had turned off the burner on the stove, so she opened doors and windows and allowed fresh air into the chalet. Judy was at the kitchen table staring blankly into space. Donna didn't disrupt her mental journey until the house was back in shape, then sat opposite Judy at the table. She reached across and took both of Judy's trembling hands and held them steady, saying nothing, just letting her love flow into Judy, not certain how much Judy was receiving. It was Judy who broke the silence. "Why, Donna?" she asked, raising her eyes to meet Donna's.

"God alone knows, Judy," Donna said, offering no advice or religious platitudes.

"I'm a danger to myself," Judy said. "I can't remember even common things like buttering the bread for a grilled cheese sandwich. Half of the time I don't remember what I am supposed to do next."

"Is this what happens with Huntington's?" Donna asked, knowing the answer.

"This and much more," Judy answered. "I really don't want to go on, Donna, but I know that that is not a topic that you want to discuss."

"We can discuss it, Judy, but you know where I stand on the issue of suicide."

"Would you feel the same way if you were me?"

"You know that I can't answer that, Judy," Donna answered. "I'll have to reserve my answer until my time comes, but I hope that I will have the strength of my convictions. I pray that the Spirit will give me that strength."

"What should I be praying for?" Judy asked.

"The same thing. Strength, primarily, to hang on to the faith that teaches that there is something better after this life."

"What about praying for a cure?"

"Of course. I pray for that every day for you, but I also recognize that one way or another we will all die and need the assurance that death is not the end of life. For those who believe, death is a transition to a new life— a better life where there is no such thing as Huntington's. In a way, the transition is like birth. An unborn baby is protected, comfortable in her mother's body, being nourished and served by her mother. She doesn't know what to expect from life, but what she does know is that the transition to life outside of her mother will be painful for both. Not until they have gone through the pain and mess of childbirth can the baby experience the wonder of life outside of her mother's womb. You and I are in the womb of this life. We can't know what is ahead for us in the next life until we have passed through the uncertainty and pain of death—through the valley, so to speak. We will go through death in our own way, but the outcome will be the same for all of us who believe—that the next life will bring no pain, and no more death."

"What is wrong, then, with speeding up the process? What would God do if that happened?" Judy asked.

"I can't speak for God, Judy," Donna said. "But God says that He knows all of our days before the first one came to be, and I can't imagine that He would be pleased if you took that matter into your own hands."

Donna stayed with Judy until Mark returned from his first full day as a Ranger trainee, then said goodbye. Mark shared his experiences with Judy. She was eager to hear about his adventures. When it came her turn to share, Mark realized that her day had not gone as well.

"A package arrived today from Festival Cruise Lines," Judy said while Mark was climbing out of his fatigues. He pulled on a sweat suit and slippers, then carried the package into the living room. The package was a binder with a colorful label reading, "Welcome to Festival Cruise Lines." Included were detailed instructions on what to bring and what not to bring, an itinerary for their travel to Miami, and instructions on how to identify the shuttle service at the airport. There were suggestions on what to wear and a reservation form for choosing the early or late meal hour, which they completed immediately, opting for early. There were also brochures describing the activities available at the ports where they could disembark as well as activities on board.

15

The two detectives assigned to the Bio-Gen case barged into Captain Gordon's office without knocking. "We just got word from the crime scene folks that they can't seal the lab. Did you know that the lab was being rebuilt?"

"No," Gordon replied. "I know that the Arson Investigator released the lab when he closed his investigation, but I didn't expect Bio-Gen to move that quickly to repair the damage. Is anything left?"

"Not much," the lead investigator answered. "The damaged equipment has been removed and the room is being gutted. If there's a case to build, it's going to be without the lab."

Louise called Keith Lawson, again at home. After pleasantries, she said, "You didn't tell me that the lab was being repaired. There's no way that we can build a case without the lab."

"Louise, the lab was unchanged two days ago. I went by there myself. If repair work is being done, it was started in the last two days, probably since the police took the tapes."

"Someone is covering their tracks," Louise said. "I'll get back to you, Keith. I have to have time to think. It would be helpful if you could stop by my office tomorrow."

"Could we do this over lunch, Louise?"

"Sure, same place as last time?" Louise asked.

Both arrived at the storefront Chinese restaurant at the same time. After assembling their meal from the buffet, they chose a booth away from the front windows. "Keith, there is only one way that we are going to get the evidence that we need, and you're not going to like it," Louise warned.

"What?"

"You're going to have to get Krimer to implicate himself," Louise answered.

"You've been watching too many Law and Order shows," Keith said. "You don't do those things in real life, do you, Louise?"

"Not very often. Only when we're desperate. The crime scene is no more, Keith. We have motive. You said that the scientists had information that could damage Bio-Gen. We have the CEO staging the event. But we don't have enough to move from accident or carelessness to homicide. I need for you to record a confession."

"This sounds like a TV script. You want me to wear a recorder?" Keith asked.

"Yes, and it's no TV script. It's for real, and it has real risks," Louise warned.

"Such as? You don't think that Krimer is going to pull out his silenced pistol and plug me, do you?" Keith asked with a smile.

"You don't seem to be taking this very seriously, Keith. If you're right about this, this is a man who arranged the murder, and I'll say it again, *murder*, of two of your employees. Don't think that he's not capable of doing it again just because he wears a white shirt. What do you think he'll do if he discovers that you are responsible for this investigation?"

"I get the message, Louise. How does this work?" Keith asked.

"It's simple. It's not like the old movies. Recording devices today are almost undetectable. We'll be in the parking lot of Bio-Gen probably in a borrowed utility truck receiving and recording the sound. We'll also be seconds away if you get into trouble, but I don't expect that. All you have to do is get Krimer to implicate himself."

"What am I supposed to say?" Keith asked. "Did you plan the murder of Palmer and Phillips?"

"Obviously you can't be that blunt. I'll get a police psychologist to coach you, Keith, but you will have to improvise. You're sharp, Keith. You'll find the words to say. We'll help. Will you do it?"

"Okay. I'm afraid that I'll be so nervous that he'll see right through me."

"Our psychologist will help you with that, too. Can you meet her today?" Louise asked.

"No, I can't. Is tomorrow okay?" Keith said. Gordon called the psychologist and an appointment was set for a meeting with Louise and Keith.

Keith was surprised when the police psychologist walked into Captain Gordon's office. She was petite, brunette, twenty-ish, and stylishly dressed. Aware of Keith's assessment, she extended her hand, introduced herself, then staged the seating arrangement, assigning Louise Gordon to a chair in the corner of her own office, placing Keith in a chair at the side of Louise's desk, then sitting in Louise's desk chair. "You're going to record a conversation with your boss, is that correct?" she said without any pleasantries.

"Yes."

"Louise, what will he be using?" the psychologist asked. Louise described the device and explained how it would be used, where the sound would be received and recorded, and the legal permission that had been secured to gain the evidence. "Do you have any reservations, Mr. Lawson?" the psychologist asked.

"Of course, wouldn't you?"

"Probably, but I'm not the one doing the job. May I make some suggestions?"

"That's why we're here," Keith said, getting annoyed with the impersonal way that the interview was being handled. He expected coaching, not bullying.

"Okay, first I suggest that the setting be natural. Do you have any meetings scheduled with your boss?" the psychologist asked.

"Yes, the executives meet regularly."

"When is the next meeting?"

"Tomorrow, actually," Keith answered, "at 10:00 A.M."

"Can we be ready in a day?" the psychologist asked, turning to Louise Gordon.

"Yes, if Keith is ready," Louise said.

"Okay. You understand the objective, right, Mr. Lawson?"

"Yes, to get the CEO to implicate himself in the killings," he answered.

"Right, but we don't want you to force the issue. It may take several meetings to get what we want," the psychologist said. "Is there a segue that will open a conversation about the killings?"

"The police confiscated some tapes at Bio-Gen. That created quite a stir. The CEO and Senior Legal Advisor have been meeting regularly," Keith suggested.

"Great. Use it, then speak in a natural tone of voice. Sometimes when we're anxious we need to increase our oxygen supply. Take a few deep breaths before speaking if you feel your adrenaline pumping, without being too obvious. Do not use words that imply that a crime has been committed until the coup de grâce, understand?" Keith nodded. The psychologist looked at Louise, "Understood?" Louise nodded. The psychologist got up and left as unceremoniously as she had entered.

"Great personality," Keith said.

"Goes with the job, I guess," Louise agreed. "Come in tomorrow at 7:00 o'clock. I'll have the techs ready then, okay?"

On the morning of the Executive Committee meeting, Keith reported to Captain Gordon's office as requested. He was tired from lack of sleep. Not wanting to disclose the plan, he had not discussed what was ahead with his wife. He was also disturbed about implicating a colleague. Keith had never been close to Aaron Krimer or even liked him on a personal level, but the man's ambition and what he had done for Bio-Gen had impressed him. It was Krimer who had been the reason that Bio-Gen received the lucrative contract with the NIH to join the Human Genome Project. That contract put Bio-Gen on the map. Losing the contract was unacceptable, at any cost. Keith Lawson had no ambitions to be anything more than what he was—a Chief Financial Officer for a reputable company. Krimer had jeopardized that reputation by his actions, and Keith had no hesitation to do what Captain Gordon asked if it meant reestablishing the integrity of Bio-Gen. "Good morning, Keith," Louise Gordon said as she stepped into the elevator on her way to the police technical lab.

"Good morning, Louise," he replied.

"Sleep well?" she asked with a smile.

"Right," Keith said, glancing at Louise from the corner of his eyes.

"It will be over soon," she said, hoping that she was correct. "All you have to do is give us cause to arrest him."

"How will that work?" Keith asked.

"As I said before, we'll be listening to your conversation. As soon as the CEO says anything that implicates himself in the killings, we will move to the conference room and place him in custody."

They reached the floor of the tech lab and walked to the surveillance cubicle. Two technicians were waiting for them. It took only a few minutes for them to place the microphone receiver and transmitter on Keith. Keith had had visions of black boxes strapped to his body, but was amazed at how small the equipment was and how inconspicuous it appeared. "That's the easy part," Louise said. "Now we get to test it." The technicians left the lab, went to the parking lot in front of the precinct station and entered a van borrowed from KC's Electric Supply Co., a company owned by one of the techs. After ten minutes had passed, they returned and rejoined Keith and Louise in the lab. Inserting a cassette-sized tape into a common cassette player, Keith was amazed to hear with clarity the conversation he had just had with Louise while they waited.

"Better take care of your toilet needs before we turn you on, Keith, or we'll be listening to that, too," Louise said.

Keith arrived at Bio-Gen as usual at 9:00 A.M. He greeted the receptionist and his secretary, then conferred with him to review the day's activities. At 9:45 he took the elevator to the third floor and stopped in the men's room on the way to the meeting. Just before leaving he activated the equipment attached to his sport coat. As directed, he spoke a few words into the equipment before leaving the men's room, then waited. If the equipment was working, no one would come up to the men's room from the van. If not, a tech would enter the men's room within ten minutes. No one came. At 9:55 Keith entered the conference room. Rory Sanders and Aaron Krimer were already seated. After formalities and department reports were concluded, Keith asked, "Has there been any further activity from the Chicago Police Department regarding our security tapes?" The COO and CEO glanced at each other, and then Krimer spoke to Keith.

"We're leaving that matter to the legal department, Keith. Why do you ask?"

"Why do I ask?" Keith said, feigning indignation. "This is a matter of some concern to this committee, I would think. What exactly were they looking for?"

"As I said, Keith, this is a matter for the legal department. I suppose that you are entitled to an explanation, although I don't see where this effects the Finance Department at present. They were continuing their investigation of the deaths in Lab 311."

"It was my impression that the Arson Investigator closed that investigation," Keith said.

"The Fire Department is not involved at present, Keith. Is there any further business for this meeting?" Krimer asked, looking back and forth at Sanders and Lawson.

"Come on, Keith, keep it going," Louise Gordon said to the lab tech seated next to her in the van. "Don't make us do this again."

"Who then is interested?" Keith asked, not willing to lose the opportunity.

"The police took the tapes," Krimer said abruptly, standing to leave.

"Then they are suspecting something more than an accident?" Keith persisted.

Krimer glared at Keith. "You are entering into dangerous territory, Keith. It would serve you well to drop the topic."

"There's no reason for raised voices, gentlemen," Sanders interjected. "I'm certain that their investigation will not find anything."

Krimer hissed at Sanders to remain silent, then, pointing a finger at Keith, he said, "What is your interest in this, Keith?"

Keith began to feel his heart beat quicken, and felt as though the technical equipment that was recording the meeting was pinned to the front of his face. "Isn't this the Executive Committee? Aren't we the directing body of this organization? Whatever pertains to one, pertains to all. Either we are a team or we aren't," Keith asserted.

"Attaboy," Louise said with a raised fist.

"Don't you lecture me, Lawson" Krimer said through a closed jaw and narrowed eyes. "If you were a team player, you wouldn't be asking these questions. You would know what it takes to run a company. You wouldn't be pushing pencils on the sideline. You'd be up front like Sanders and I making the tough decisions."

"Such as?" Keith said, taking an offensive posture.

He had pushed Krimer to the breaking point. "Such as making damn sure that two scientists don't destroy everything that we've done in this company." Sanders jumped to his feet and moved between the two combatants.

"No, step aside," Krimer said. "Let's see what kind of team player this number cruncher is. Palmer and Phillips were all that stood between us and a miracle drug that will make this company a legend. Do you think that Sanders and I were about to be vulnerable to them?"

"Don't tell me that you two had something to do with their so-called accident," Keith persisted.

"Get the men ready to move," Louise said to the detective in the van.

"I'm not telling you another thing," Krimer said. "Now understand this—if you say a word about this conversation to anyone, the Chicago Police Department may have another investigation on their hands, do I make myself clear?"

"I will not be threatened," Keith said. "Nor will I be part of any organization that solves its problems by killing its employees."

"He's getting himself in too deep," Louise said. "We've got to get him out of there. Move now!" A squad of four men, including the detective in charge of the Bio-Gen case began to head for the building. Louise and the technicians continued recording the activities in the conference room.

"Don't put yourself on the firing line, Keith," Sanders said. "We can work this out if we will all just calm down. What we did had to be done. We would all have been ruined. Try to understand."

"What you did was murder," Keith repeated.

"Call it what you want, but keep it to yourself," Krimer demanded as the door to the conference room flew open and three uniformed men burst into the room. The detective in a business suit had not been authorized to make an arrest, so he ordered the men to stand and place their hands on the table. Two uniformed officers patted them down and nodded to the detective.

"Sit down, gentlemen," the detective commanded. All three executives complied.

"I demand to know what this is all about," Krimer said.

"You can demand all you want," Louise Gordon said as she entered the room. "Take these two into custody," she said to the detective, pointing to Sanders and Krimer. "We'll file charges at the station."

"Charges for what?" Krimer demanded.

"How does murder sound for starters?" Louise said as the two men were handcuffed. "Well done, Mr. Lawson," she said to Keith.

"You bastard," Krimer said to Keith. "You set us up. You better stay awake nights."

"That's enough," Sanders said to a surprised Krimer. "Keep your mouth shut."

"Any other threats you'd like to convey?" Louise asked as she motioned to the police to leave the room. The CEO and COO were unceremoniously escorted to a waiting patrol car while Keith and Louise did a high-five in the conference room. "Good job, Keith. We've got enough for an indictment, I believe."

"Thanks, Louise," Keith said, shaking Captain Gordon's hand. "Now what?"

"Now you wait until we need your testimony. The prosecutor's office will be the next people you hear from. What will you do now?"

"I will probably clear my desk for starters," Keith said.

Mark knew that Judy's death wish wasn't a ploy for attention as many are. He knew that she was tired of fighting her disease and afraid of the future. Feeling trapped between his impending loss and Judy's despair, his opposition to assisting her in her death wish was waning.

Seymour Klein was a neurologist in Berlin, New Hampshire, known to Dr. Ryan as an expert in the treatment of Huntington's disease. It was to Dr. Klein who Dr. Ryan had turned for advice for treating Judy. She arranged an appointment for Mark to see Dr. Klein for a consultation.

The medical center in Berlin surprised Mark as he turned into the parking area. He wondered why a man with Klein's reputation would be situated in a house converted into medical offices. The sign in front of the former house listed Klein, an optometrist, and a dental partnership. Klein's entrance was at the side of the house. He was surprised again when he entered the office. There was no receptionist or waiting area, just an office. Dr. Klein rose, greeted Mark, then directed him to a conversation grouping of upholstered chairs in front of his desk. His office was a mess. Files were stacked on his desk, each bulging with papers arranged helter-skelter. His walls were lined with bookshelves, and except for sets, the books were lying on their sides or standing askew. Klein himself fit in with his office. He was unshaven, casually dressed, albeit stylishly, and in stocking feet. As he guided Mark to the chairs he offered a glass of water, which Mark accepted, then found that his pitcher was empty. While he left the office to refill the pitcher, Mark sat wondering whether he had made the right decision.

Klein returned and poured water for both of them, then sat opposite Mark. Klein appeared to be in his early sixties, had a full head of hair through which a comb had been hastily pulled, wore trifocals in need of cleaning, and had a salt and pepper goatee and mustache. Of average size, he appeared to be well toned, perhaps a cyclist or runner, certainly in better shape than most men his age. "Dr. Ryan called," he said. "So you're the husband of the lady she has been treating for Huntington's." Mark didn't know whether that was a statement or a question.

"My wife is Judy Garrison."

"And you are here because?"

"Because she is set on ending her life," Mark answered, "and she wants me to help."

"And what do you want me to say to you, Mr. Garrison?" Mark was startled at the question. He really didn't know what he wanted to hear. The doctor interrupted Mark's thoughts. "I suppose you want me to tell you that it is okay for the two of you to end your wife's life. Well, I won't. On the other hand, what I will tell you is this. The time is coming, if Dr. Ryan's prognosis is correct, when your wife—Judy, isn't it?—will no longer be able to make those decisions for herself. If my information is correct, and it usually is, Judy has witnessed the later stages of Huntington's in her father.

She is also declining a little faster than usual, according to Dr. Ryan, and is tired of losing control. This is an expected complication of Huntington's—the desire to end it all. It is why we send patients and their families for counseling. I'm not sure whether the counseling makes any difference, but we do it mainly so that if they do end the life of the patient, they will understand the consequences—legal and emotional. Be clear, I will not advise you, assist you, or discourage you. The decision is yours and Judy's—that's her name, right?—but you will have only this window of opportunity and you will need to make a decision and stick with it."

"I'm not entirely clear on what you mean—this window of opportunity."

"Pay attention, young man. I don't like to repeat myself," the doctor said in a kindly tone. Mark was not insulted and was strangely drawn to the doctor. "Your wife's brain is being destroyed by a genetic monster. She is losing her ability to think. Is that clear to you?" He didn't wait for Mark to respond. "In another six months, I would guess, she will barely recognize you and will not be able to initiate any action on her own behalf. Again, do I make myself clear?"

Mark was clear. "Yes, sir."

"Good, now understand this. The legal, moral, religious, or medical implications of assisted suicide mean nothing to me. What matters is that we are dealing with a damned miserable disease that leaves people like me feeling helpless, and if I feel helpless, I can't imagine how you and your wife feel. Much is being done to find a way to end this plague, but we aren't there yet and won't be, barring a miracle, before Judy dies, however that happens. You came to me for advice and I have none, except to say that you must listen to your wife while she is able to form thoughts and communicate them. After that you will be on your own. I'm truly sorry that I can't help you, sir." Klein rose, walked to Mark's side, and put his arms around Mark's shoulder, then wept. Mark was stunned. He didn't know how to respond. Uncharacteristically, he wrapped his big arms around the older man until he pulled himself together.

"Thank you, sir," Mark said as he walked toward the door. "Is there someone who would like to see my insurance information?"

"No charge," the doctor said abruptly, then sat down behind his desk, dismissing Mark with a wave of his hand. As Mark began his long drive home, he wasn't quite certain what had happened. What stuck in his mind was the doctor's phrase "window of opportunity."

16

As the date for the cruise approached, Mark and Judy met with Dr. Ryan. She wrote prescriptions for Judy's medicine and for motion sickness patches for both, although Mark protested that he would not need the patch. She also arranged with the Woodsville Pharmacy to lend Judy a collapsible four-point walker for the cruise. Now it was Judy's turn to protest.

"Please don't spend too much time in the sun, Judy," Dr. Ryan advised. "Several of your medications make you a little more susceptible to problems. In any case, take a good sunblocker and a wide-brimmed hat."

"Are you sure I won't need to go in an ambulance?" Judy asked.

"These are extra precautions to make sure that you have a great time," Dr. Ryan replied.

"What about the flights, Dr. Ryan?" Mark asked.

"What about them?"

"Should we be making special arrangements with the airlines?" Mark asked.

"Like what?"

"I'm not sure," Mark said.

"Why not ship me in the cargo hold?" Judy asked, disturbed that the conversation was going around her. "I haven't flown in years and I'm looking forward to it. Mark, I'm a good traveler. You know that. You may need to cut up my food and help me eat it. That's no big deal for me, although it might be embarrassing for you. If I don't eat or drink too much, I won't need to use the airplane bathrooms. We'll get by."

"It won't be embarrassing, Judy," Mark said.

"Let's make an adventure out of it, Mark."

"Sounds like a plan," Ryan said, standing. She handed Judy an envelope containing a summary of her medical record for the ship's doctor, just in case. "I want you guys to have a great vacation. Send me a post card." Mark and Judy left the office bound for Woodsville Pharmacy.

Returning from a day of shopping at Steeplegate Mall in Concord Heights, Mark said, "Are you as excited about the cruise as I am?"

Judy didn't answer. He asked again. Still, she didn't answer. They were sitting in the screened-in porch enjoying the lengthening evenings and listening to the birds settle in for the night. "It's beautiful here in the woods, Mark. Will you stay here after I die?"

"I don't know, Judy, what I'll do when the time comes."

"I'd like to think of you being here and working with Dave and remembering our life, but I know that you will find someone and begin a new life. I want you to know, Mark, that it would be a great disappointment to me if you didn't have a happy life."

"You've given me more happiness than any man deserves," Mark said

"I know, Mark," Judy continued, "but you have to think about the future. This cruise will be my last hurrah. You know that. You should plan accordingly."

"What do you mean 'your last hurrah'?" Mark asked.

"I had a dream about the man who fell overboard during the Kraft's cruise. He was saved, I know. In my dream I also saw myself falling into the clear, cold water and sinking slowly into the darkness as my mind lapsed quietly into unconsciousness. Isn't that the way drowning is described?"

"I've read that, Judy, but that was a dream. This is reality."

"My reality is short-lived no matter how I die, Mark."

"What are you telling me, Judy?" Mark asked, knowing but not wanting to hear the answer.

"I'm getting tired, Mark," Judy said, not wanting to continue the conversation. "We have to leave in two days and I haven't begun to pack. Donna is coming early tomorrow to help me. We should probably go to bed. You may not have noticed, but I'm wearing White Shoulders." Mark got the message and helped Judy up the short flight of stairs to the bedroom passageway. They made love and fell asleep in each other's arms.

The next day, while Mark and Dave worked on the Trail, Donna stayed with Judy. She made breakfast and watched the local news on TV. "Hi, Sleepyhead," she said as Judy staggered to the top of the stairs. "Ready for French toast?"

"You bet," Judy answered. The women discussed packing over breakfast. Afterward, Donna brought the new luggage into the master bedroom, then emailed Mark and Judy's itinerary to Lois and Donald Douglas while Judy rummaged her drawers for clothes to pack. Together they picked Judy's clothes and toiletries, fantasizing about what she would be doing on board the cruise. When they were finished, they went into the living room. "I want you to have this," Judy said, holding out a small box to Donna.

"What is this?"

"Open it and you'll see," Judy said. Donna opened the box. Inside was a collection of jewelry including pearl earrings, a turquoise bracelet, and a crystal necklace.

"What is the occasion, Judy?" Donna asked.

"You are my best friend," Judy answered, "and I don't have any daughters to pass things along to. The earrings and bracelet were my grandmothers and the necklace belonged to my mother. I want you to have them while I can still remember who you are."

Donna stood and walked to Judy's recliner. She knelt, then sat in front of Judy and lay her head on Judy's lap. With tears pouring down her cheeks, she wrapped her arms around Judy's legs and cried while Judy watched. After a few minutes, she looked up at Judy and said, "I love you, Judy. Thank you for these gifts. I will cherish them always." She closed the box, expecting, but not saying that this was a gesture of goodbye. Feelings collided in her mind between accepting the intentions of her friend and pleading for her life on any grounds—religious or otherwise, but knowing that she could not control the outcome, and would have to accept it.

After packing their luggage in the Excursion, Mark said. "Let's hit the road. You've got the ship phone number and our cell phone numbers, right Dave? And you've got the itinerary, Donna?"

"For the fourth time, Mark, yes," Donna answered. "Now quit worrying and go have a cruise." Dave helped Mark load the luggage into the Excursion, and then they all waved back-and-forth until the SUV was out of sight. The Kraft's closed up the chalet and headed home.

"You've been awfully quiet this morning," Dave said to Donna. "Is everything okay?"

"Of course," Donna answered without explanation.

Judy fared well on the flights. Although there were four flights, there were only two plane changes. A two-hour layover in Boston and another in Atlanta allowed plenty of time for leisurely meals. She ate light and had no need to use the airplane facilities. Cramped seating, safety belts, and tranquilizers kept her spasms in check. During the two-hour flights she slept while Mark read Festival literature.

Mark and Judy couldn't believe their eyes when their shuttle delivered them to the dock. The ship was enormous—a huge floating hotel. It was behind a large warehouse-type building. Roping guided arriving passengers down a corridor, then up stairs to the check-in area, a large open area with a long counter. Stations were arranged by letters. The Garrisons headed for the G-H-I station where they were processed. Baggage was passed over the counter, then disappeared down a conveyor belt with the promise that it would appear next in their cabin. They displayed all the right credentials and were issued their Festival Fun Card—a combination credit card and debark/embark pass—with the caution that it should remain with them at all times.

Roping guided them again to the rear of the warehouse where they stepped out into the midday sunlight of Miami just long enough to walk into a covered gangway, and then onto the ship. Crewmembers greeted them with a smile and directed them to their cabin. There were four cabin decks. Mark had paid extra for a cabin on the outside of the ship and on the highest cabin deck so that they would have fewer stairs to negotiate during the cruise. It was called the Princess Deck. Their cabin was P314. They were pleasantly surprised as they stepped inside.

The sun shone through a spotted and smeared window about three feet high and four feet wide. The cabin was somewhat larger than Mark or Judy had expected and they were pleased. A card on each bed introduced Marina as the cabin crewmember that would be responsible for maintaining their cabin. Judy was pleased that there was no wave motion until Mark reminded her that they were still in port. Embarkation was an hour away.

Just as they were about to leave the cabin to explore the ship, a loud and clear announcement came over a speaker hidden somewhere in the room. It was preceded by three NBC-type tones. "Welcome to Festival Cruise Lines. The first activity on-board today will be an emergency drill scheduled to take place approximately one hour after we leave port." After the drill announcement, they were advised to consult the TV or the daily Festival newsletter for each day's activities.

As they prepared to leave the cabin, there was a knock. Marina was standing in the corridor with their luggage. She was Latin, beautiful, and bubbly, and would become a valuable source of information during the cruise. Mark moved the luggage into the cabin, then he and Judy squeezed past several luggage jams on their corridor to reach the steps going up to the lowest of three activity decks. Reaching the Florence Deck, they moved at once to the ship's rail, then followed the rail to the bow from where they could see the channel leading to the sea.

There was excitement everywhere. Novice cruisers like Mark and Judy were studying Festival literature. Veterans were checking out the lounges and casino. Families with young children were exploring the swimming pools. Teens who had ditched their parents were congregating at the Pizzeria. Seniors were strolling the upper decks studying the structure of the ship. There was something for everyone. As long as she walked slowly, Judy was able to use Mark's arm rather than the four-point walker, but she knew that she would need the walker when the ship left port. Even though they weren't moving, the ship was in the water after all and one could feel the difference.

They followed the outer rail around the entire ship on the Florence Deck passing the on-board boutique, photo salon, casino, open-air buffet-style restaurant, two lounges and a dance club, coffee bar, and a children's swimming pool.

The rest of the first day was spent in wonderment. They completed their tour of the remaining activity decks discovering two more swimming pools, a pizza restaurant, a communications center including an Internet café, a gym, spa, and jogging track, plus observation decks on each end of the ship. What most impressed Judy was their first formal meal. The Garrisons were assigned to the Neapolitan Dining Room, table 104, at the early hour. Dress ranged from casual to semi-formal. Table 104 accommodated eight, but only six were present at the first meal. Seth was their senior server and like the other servers was well trained and personable. The guests could eat at their assigned table for every meal while they were on-board, or they could opt to eat elsewhere. Mark and Judy opted for formal for their first meal. Seth assured Mark that his request for special preparation of Judy's meal would be taken care of, and he kept his promise. After their first dinner, they returned to their cabin to check the closed circuit TV for special activities scheduled for the next day. It would be a day at sea.

On their first night at sea they slept soundly. Mark was up when Judy awoke, reading the Festival newsletter that had been slipped under their door during the night. The activities scheduled for the day included an orientation about Grand Cayman Island, a tour of the galley, a golf clinic, various game shows in the showplace lounge, an art auction, and many more activities.

It took an hour for Judy's medications to kick in and for her to get dressed with Mark's help. She wore a pair of short shorts, a tee shirt, and Nike shoes without socks. Mark rubbed sunblocker on her exposed parts, then suggested another activity, which Judy coyly deferred until the end of the day. She was grimace-free, and ready to enjoy her day. They skipped the galley tour, but Mark entered a golf putting contest and won. Judy watched from a chair. A quiz-show junkie, she said, "I'd like to go to the Jeopardy game in the showplace lounge." The emcee was a standup comic who kept the crowd in stitches.

The day passed quickly and the only couple that showed up at table 104 for dinner was the couple that had been missing the night before, a young couple obviously on their honeymoon. They introduced themselves and quickly became friends with Mark and Judy.

"Would you like to join us after dinner for a drink in the dance lounge?" they asked.

"Yes, that would be great," Mark said. After dinner the four agreed to meet in one hour at the dance lounge. On their way to their cabin, Mark and Judy passed by the communication kiosk and picked up a *Chicago Sunday Tribune*, now several days old. While Judy watched the closed circuit TV from her bed, Mark read the newspaper. After a few minutes he stood up, turned down the TV volume, and said, "Listen to this, Judy." Then he read a headline article on the front page of the business section.

BIO-GEN EXECS INDICTED
FOR MURDER.

A Cook County Grand Jury voted today to indict the Chief Executive Officer and Chief Operating Officer of Bio-Gen Laboratories on six criminal counts including two counts of first-degree murder. Both have been charged with the killing of two scientists in what had previously been ruled an act of carelessness following an arson investigation. The investigation was reopened at the request of the Chicago Police Department following the discovery of information previously undisclosed. The Grand Jury determined that the explosion and fire that took the lives of Drs. George Palmer and Michele Phillips was staged. Both executives are now being held without bond in county facilities.

A spokesman for the company announced that the Chief Financial Officer, Mr. Keith Lawson, has been appointed acting Chief Executive Officer pending the outcome of the upcoming trial. Mr. Lawson told investors in a communication issued immediately after the indictment that he expects the company to move forward without interruption, and has promised to assemble a leadership team that will earn the trust of investors and keep Bio-Gen's commitment to innovative genetic discovery.

Mark paused and looked at Judy. She had raised herself to a half-reclining, half-sitting position on the bed, but said nothing. "What do you think, honey," Mark asked.

"I don't want to think about it, Mark. Bio-Gen is cursed. My husband

and his partner, who became my friend, and now his boss and another scientist have all died unnecessary deaths. I suppose that these executives will also die or spend their lives in prison. That makes six and for what? Who knows?"

"Do you still want to go to the dance lounge?" Mark asked.

"Of course, why not?" Judy answered. They had dressed casually for dinner and had no need to change for the dance lounge. "We won't be able to dance, you know. I'm sorry."

"I already thought of that," Mark said.

"And we won't be able to drink either," Judy added, regretting to herself that this would not be like the nights spent in their living room clutching one another and rocking to the soft tones of Johnny Mathis.

"Well, we can drink, Judy, but we will have to try something new," Mark said.

"Like Shirley Temple's?" Judy said, smiling.

"Like Shirley Temple's," Mark confirmed, also smiling. He helped her to her feet, lifted her chin, and then kissed her lightly on the forehead. She pulled his head in closer, then kissed him passionately. Slowly, clumsily, she unbuttoned his shirt, then unfastened his belt. Mark responded by unbuttoning Judy's dress and letting it fall to the floor. "Did Shirley Temple do this?" he whispered as he sat on the edge of the bed while Judy held his head to her breasts.

"I hope so," Judy answered, her breath coming more rapidly. Mark lay back on the bed and Judy removed his pants and shoes, then lay next to him. They made love with abandon, forgetting Bio-Gen, Huntington's, life without dancing, and all the ills of the world, but immersing themselves in the sensations of the moment. When they were both spent, they lay quietly. After awhile Mark sat up and turned to look out the undraped window at the black night. The sea and the night were one—just blackness, no stars or moon. He raised Judy to a sitting position and she pulled her body next to his. She looked out of the window for several minutes, then said, "Let's go to the top deck."

"We should stop at the dance lounge and apologize," Mark said.

"Okay, but then I'd like to go to the top deck," she insisted. They showered, redressed and left their cabin around 9:30 P.M.

"I think that you should have your walker," Mark said. "The sea is a little more active." Judy could feel the gentle rolling of the ship, but thought that she could make it with Mark's help. "Suppose I just carry it folded," he compromised. She agreed. They returned to the cabin and Mark retrieved the walker, folded it flat, and carried it slightly behind his left arm with Judy on his right.

As they approached the entrance to the dance lounge they saw their table partners sitting with another couple obviously enjoying themselves. "I don't think that we have to interrupt them," Mark said. "They seem to be having a good time. We'll apologize at breakfast." They passed by the lounge and walked slowly to the elevator, punching the button for the Sun Deck. When they departed the elevator they were standing under a roof that extended only a few feet. Beyond was an open deck that stretched one-third the length of the ship at the bow end. No one was in sight. From where they stood they could see only the top of the massive exhaust stack to the rear, and the black night on both sides. This was obviously where passengers could come to bask in the sun of the day. White plastic chaise lounges were in various positions and scattered randomly around the deck. The light that lit the elevator platform and the adjacent stairway was the only illumination on the deck and cast eerie shadows over the open area. "Shall we return to our cabin?" Mark asked.

Judy seemed transfixed. She didn't respond to Mark's question, but staggered alone to a chaise lounge a few feet away, then sat on the edge peering out at the sea. Mark had moved quickly to help her, but she escaped his grasp. He dragged another lounge to where she was and sat facing her. "What is it?" he asked knowing that Judy was somewhere else in her thoughts.

"I love you, Mark," she said.

"I love you, too, Judy," he replied.

"Listen, Mark, to the sea," she said, turning away from him and facing the deck rail. From the twelfth deck they could barely hear voices. The only clear sounds were the sounds of the waves and the occasional shuffling of chaise lounges blown by the balmy wind. "It's calling to me, Mark. Help me to the railing." Mark unfolded the four-point walker and placed it in front of Judy, then helped her to her feet. Without his help she walked slowly surrounded by the railings of the walker until they reached the edge of the deck. From the sun deck they could look straight down to the sea. The tops of the waves close to the ship were visible from the cabin lights below. "I want to be alone, Mark."

"You know that I can't leave you alone, Judy," he said.

"I need to do this, Mark," she insisted turning her head toward Mark. He could see in her eyes that this was non-negotiable.

"Are you sure that this is what you want, Judy?" he asked, his throat tightening.

"I've never been more certain of anything," she said. She leaned toward Mark and laid her head on his chest, then said, "Please, Mark." Mark turned away from Judy and walked toward the elevator. At the elevator he turned back and stood watching Judy, who was leaning on her walker at the edge of the Sun Deck. The elevator door opened and he stepped inside.

Mark emerged from the elevator on the Princess Deck and walked to P-314. He was surprised at his own calmness. He fully understood what had happened on the Sun Deck, and he was emotionally and mentally prepared, but the reality didn't explode inside him until he walked through his cabin door and saw Judy's things. In a panic, he turned and ran from the cabin to the stairs leading up to the Sun Deck. After running up five flights of stairs two at a time, he burst through the stairway door. Neither Judy nor her walker were anywhere in sight. He fell back against the door and slid to the deck, his head in his hands. With no one in sight, he experienced a complete meltdown of feelings. Gripped by grief, anger, guilt, and intense loneliness, he shouted at the top of his lungs to no one in particular, but facing heavenward. With his fists he pounded the deck, then lay on the flat surface and sobbed uncontrollably. Then, a wave of calm came over him. Wiping his face, he stepped toward the elevator door and pushed the button for the Main Deck.

At the Main Deck, Mark approached the Purser's counter. A sleepy uniformed woman greeted him with a smile. "Can you book a flight from Grand Cayman to Boston for tomorrow?" he asked. She nodded.

"Will you be leaving the cruise?" she asked.

"Yes," Mark answered. She explained the terms of the cruise and the procedure for leaving before the cruise returned to Miami. Mark understood. His cabin attendant would escort him to the cabstand at dockside in time for his flight.

Mark returned to P-314 at 11:45 P.M. Emotionally drained, he packed his and Judy's things in preparation for leaving the cruise the next morning at Grand Cayman Island. He tried to sleep, but sleep wouldn't come. Eventually his thoughts became a blur. He awoke to sunlight pouring through his cabin window. Looking out, he saw other cruise ships dangerously close and realized that the Festival ship was at anchor. They had arrived at Grand Cayman Island. Quickly, he showered. While he was dressing, he heard a knock. The luggage was stacked on Judy's bed, so he took the top pieces to the cabin door.

Expecting Marina, Mark opened the door and turned to reach for the luggage. When he straightened up he was looking at Judy. "I thought ...," he said, but Judy placed her hand on his mouth before he could finish.

"I know what you thought," she said. Mark moved the walker from between them and bent to pick up his wife, then carried her to the bed. Marina tapped lightly at the open door.

"I've come for your luggage," she said, reaching for the two bags near the doorway.

"The rest is here," Mark said, pointing to the other bed. "You may take them all."

"I have a statement from the Purser that you are to sign, sir," Marina said, handing an envelope to Mark. He opened the statement, made some notations, signed it, then returned it to the attendant.

"What is happening?" Judy asked softly.

"We're going home," Mark said. Judy didn't object.

17

Thirty minutes after her appearance at the cabin door, Judy was being helped by Mark into a clean, yellow taxicab at the dock on Grand Cayman Island while the dark-skinned driver loaded their luggage into the trunk. They were driven to a small airport where the largest aircraft in sight was a two-engine US Airways jet. Neither Judy nor Mark spoke for the duration of the short drive. When they were boarded and belted, Mark opened the conversation, "Do you want to talk about it?" She shook her head, closed her eyes, and slept until the aircraft landed at Miami International Airport. On the next leg of their return journey, from Miami to Atlanta, Judy asked for time when Mark tried again to get her to talk. After changing planes in Atlanta, she opened up without invitation.

They had reached cruising altitude on the leg to Logan Airport in Boston when Judy turned to Mark and said, "I saw you."

"What do you mean? Where?" Mark asked.

"On the Sun Deck," Judy replied.

"I looked for you," Mark said. "I didn't see you. I thought ..." Again, Judy wouldn't let him finish.

"I know what you thought," Judy interrupted. "A few minutes later you would have been right, but I saw you. I know that you didn't see me. I was sitting on a chaise lounge in the shadows."

"Why didn't you say something?"

"Because I was confused," she answered. "I was trying to sort things out in my mind. My head was spinning. Then I saw you, and I knew that I couldn't leave you, no matter what. I'm so sorry, Mark, for putting you through this." Her legs began to thrash about, and her head jerked to one side. Mark realized at once that she hadn't taken her medications, which were now in her luggage. He pressed the button above his head to call the Flight Attendant. He came at once.

"My wife's medicine was checked in with her luggage. She has Huntington's Disease and needs a tranquilizer to calm her. Can you help?" The attendant excused himself and promised to return.

"Can you tell me what your wife is taking?" he asked upon returning. Mark identified the drug that Judy took for spasms. In a few minutes an announcement was made over the speaker system appealing to any passenger who may have carried that drug on-board. It wasn't long before the attendant returned with a single dose of Judy's medicine. Within thirty minutes, her body was relaxed and she dozed. Again, Mark pushed the call button for the Flight Attendant.

"Is there a pharmacy at Logan Airport?" he asked.

"Yes, there is one in the retail shops near the ticket counters," the attendant answered. With the attendant's permission, Mark called Dr. Ryan's office from his cell phone and asked the receptionist to have the doctor call the Logan Airport pharmacy to order a single dose of all of Judy's medications for their pickup within two hours. In a matter of minutes, she returned to say that it would be done.

"I want to talk about it, Mark," she said, sitting up straight in her seat. She looked straight ahead at the back of the passenger seat in front of her. "I guess you could say that the cruise was the last straw, " she began. "It made me realize that the only place left for me is where I can be cared for until I die. That didn't seem like enough. I'm not ready to die, Mark, but when we passed by the dance lounge and watched the other couples I realized that I can't have that and the worst part is that as long as I am alive I am keeping you from enjoying life. Don't say anything, Mark. I know you love me and will tell me that being with me is all that you want, but you don't know how much guilt that puts on me. I don't want your love at any price, and the price that we are about to pay is a high one. It seemed to me that the simplest solution would be for me to jump overboard, breathe deeply, and take a peaceful sleep." She turned toward Mark and looked into his eyes.

"But you didn't" he said, pausing for her to continue.

"No, I didn't, and you may wish someday that I had."

"You already know how I feel, Judy," he said.

"You don't know what you are saying, Mark," she replied. "Spend time with Lois. Listen to her story. Talk to others who have cared for Huntington's patients. You are in for a rough ride." Mark remained silent. "But it wasn't for you alone that I changed my mind. I couldn't dismiss what Donna said, not once, but several times—that my life does not belong to me. And it doesn't belong to you either, Mark. It belongs to God. He gave me biological life and baptismal life, and someday He will give me eternal life. While I was sitting on the Sun Deck listening to the waves and the wind, I had the sense that I wasn't alone, that someone was there with me. When you left me, you thought that you were giving me control over my life. It was the highest respect that you could have shown me, Mark, and I will always remember that. But I don't have control over my life. 'All authority in heaven and on earth has been given to me,' Jesus said. I have Huntington's and I have to accept that. Donna reminded me of what Saint Paul said about having all knowledge in eternity. Perhaps I will know then why I have to die in this way. Or perhaps it won't matter then. We all die sooner or later. All that I could do on the Sun Deck was listen to the waves and the wind, knowing that behind them or in them I heard a small voice saying 'You belong to me.' Then the door to the stairwell opened and you appeared and I saw your brokenness. In it I realized what I had done to you, and my decision was made. You have been my strength since the first time we met, when you came to my front door to tell me that Bob's body had been found in the Des Plaines River. You have always been my strength, and now I need you more than ever." There was no emotion in Judy's voice, just commitment from the depth of her being. Mark held her quivering hand, and they sat together without speaking.

After awhile he said, "I'm glad you're back. Nothing will ever separate us, Judy, not even death."

The remaining flights were uneventful. Both were tired when they arrived at the chalet, but at peace as they faced the future. "Should we call Dave and Donna?" Judy asked as Mark helped her through the front door.

"Let's not call them until tomorrow," Mark replied. The telephone in the chalet was on the kitchen counter, not immediately visible from the front door. Mark unloaded the luggage from the Excursion while Judy rested on the recliner in the living room. The chalet was cold so Mark had covered her with a small blanket. When he was finished, Mark adjusted the thermostat. It was then that he saw the telephone. The red light was flashing and the digital screen indicated that there was one call recorded. Mark picked up the handset and pushed the button labeled "play."

The speaker was obviously not pleased about recording a message. "Yes, hello," he said. "This is Seymour Klein calling for Mark Garrison. Please call me when you return. Thank you."

Judy was asleep in the recliner. Mark carried her up the few stairs to the bedroom, dressed her in flannel pajamas, put her in bed and pulled up the railings, then lay down in his bed. Judy slept until 10:30 the next morning.

After a cold breakfast of cereal and fruit, Mark called Dr. Klein. "Yes?" the doctor said sharply as a way of greeting his caller.

"Dr. Klein, this is Mark Garrison from Woodsville. You left a message on my telephone asking me to return your call."

"Garrison? Oh, yes, Garrison—with the Huntington's wife, is that it?"

"Yes," Mark replied.

"What can I do for you Mr. Garrison? I'm very busy," Klein said.

"You called me, sir," Mark said. "Was there something that you wanted me to know?"

"Wait a minute," Klein said, and the phone went silent. In a moment Klein spoke again, "I have a letter here about a new drug that is available for experimental use. Wait a minute. Yes, yes, here it says that Huntington's patients are eligible if their body weight is within sixty percent of the Metropolitan chart. How much does your wife weigh?"

"Presently, she weighs ninety-one pounds."

"How tall is she?"

"Five feet, seven inches."

"Wait a minute." Again the phone went silent. "She barely makes the weight, but it appears as though she qualifies for this new experimental drug. When can you bring her to my office?"

"Please tell me about the drug."

"Not much to tell. I told you it is experimental. That means that your wife may or may not get better, but why the questions? Do you have a better solution? I thought you would be pleased to know about it."

"Yes, yes, I am," Mark assured the doctor. "Can I bring Judy in today?"

"All right, all right, but don't bring her until after lunch."

"Can you tell me a little about the drug?" Mark persisted, wondering about side effects.

"Yes, it is being written up as a kind of cure-all. Only patients with terminal diseases are being included in the experimental program. Huntington's Disease is specifically mentioned. A laboratory called Bio-Gen has developed it. What else do you need to know? I'm very busy," Klein said.

"Nothing, sir," Mark replied. "We'll be there after lunch. Thank you." He went at once to Judy's bed to awaken her. He lowered the rails on the sides of her bed, sat on the edge of the bed and gently smoothed her blonde hair from her face. "Maybe, just maybe," he thought.

"What is it, Mark?" Judy asked as she opened her eyes and looked up at him sleepily.

"I just talked to Dr. Klein. There is a new experimental drug that he thinks we should try, and wait until you hear this. It was developed by Bio-Gen."

With her eyes shut, Judy said softly, "Thank you, God. Thank you, Bob."

Printed in the United States
21276LVS00007B/1-18